Shifting Hearts

Wiccan Haus
Book 1

By
Dominique Eastwick

This book is a work of fiction. Names, characters, places, and incidents are the products of the author's imagination or used fictitiously. Any resemblance to actual events, locales or persons, living or dead, is entirely coincidental.

Praise for *Shifting Hearts*

If you like your fantasy/paranormal/supernatural stuff with a good dose of hot romance, absolutely give Shifting Hearts a try. ~ Amazon Reviewer

Sometimes it just takes an alpha were-tiger to help you figure out what you want in life. So where do you find one? At the Wiccan Haus, of course. Just don't expect him to greet you with open arms. ~ Long and Short Reviews

I love how Ms Eastwick brings her characters to life and builds a world I would love to visit. ~ Amazon Reviewer

Hot, Hot, Hot. What an unbelievably sexy and sweet story. You can't help but fall for this one! ~ Amazon Reviewer

5 smoking hot stars out of 5. This spicy page turner *gets you hooked from the get go!* ~ Amazon Reviewer

The book grabs you from page one and doesn't let you go until the story has been told. ~ Amazon Reviewer

If Wiccan Haus Series is as good as book one all these authors are sitting on a gold mine. Ms. Eastwick has written her characters with such empathy and personalities. You automatically fall in love with them. ~ Amazon Reviewer

~A Note from the Author~

Dear Reader,

Welcome to the Wiccan Haus.

Something wiccan this way comes to a mystical, mysterious island where authors get to play and bring their love stories to life. At the Wiccan Haus you will meet Rekkus, Cyrus, Sage, Sarka, Cemil, and Myron, all of whom return in most, if not all of the stories. Yes, each one will eventually get their happily-ever-after, as well.

We hope you enjoy the stories from all the authors and return time and again to keep up with the staff and meet new characters along the way. But fear not if this is your first or twenty-first story—each book stands on its own.

Dom

Welcome to Wiccan Haus

Something wiccan this way comes to a mystical mysterious island where authors get to play and bring their love stories to life. At the Wiccan Haus you will meet Rekkus, Cyrus, Sage, Sarka, Cemil and Myron, all of whom return in most if not all the stories. Yes each one will eventually get their HEA as well.

We hope you enjoy the stories from all the authors and return time and again to keep up with the staff and meet new characters along the way. But fear not if this is your first or twenty-first story each book stands on its own. If you want to know more about the series please sign up for our newsletter.

http://thewiccanhaus.blogspot.com

Dedication

To all my Wiccan Haus sisters who help to make the Wiccan Haus a place I would want to stay at.

Chapter One

Mountains rose from their foggy curtain as the ferry approached its destination. Dana's gasp was drowned out by the others on the ferryboat. She'd known there were small islands all along the coast of Maine, but never had she expected this; an island that had appeared small in the brochure now looked immense, seeming to materialize out of nowhere. Odd, while most places used trick photography to make their resorts seem bigger, this one had done the opposite.

There were twelve of them aboard the ferry— seven women and five men. When Dana's group had boarded the ferry, twelve other, very relaxed people disembarked onto the mainland. The only thing other than her best friend, Jessie Ranata, that had kept Dana from leaving and going home were memories of those twelve people returning after a week at the mysterious resort, content and stress-free.

The ferry docked with a small nudge against the

wooden dock. The passengers waited expectantly, eager to disembark. Except Dana. She stayed to the rear, letting everyone go in front of her. Even the crew, with their boxes and coolers of supplies, got off before she did. In the end, she had no choice but to leave and took the gangplank to the dock. Throwing her bag over her shoulder, she walked toward her friend waiting for her at the end of the pier.

Dana stared at the Bavarian-style building ahead. Who would have thought there'd be a German chalet off the coast of Maine? Chalet might not be the right word, but the place could have stepped right out of a travel brochure for Oktoberfest. The large building, with its whitewashed walls, red-stained beams, and red shingles, stood out along the rocky shoreline. The sign, Wiccan Haus, completed the Germanic image.

She glanced behind her as the ferry disappeared into the fog. It didn't matter if she wanted to leave. The boat, with its silent crew, had departed. She was stuck there unless she was willing to swim. Not being a great swimmer, that didn't seem like a viable option.

Pausing, she thought about turning around and getting out of there, no matter how she had to do it. She and Frank were supposed to be in the Caribbean—married, happy, and horny. Just the two of them, spending the next week naked. Instead, she would spend it here with Jessie, her best friend in the whole wide world, but not the person she'd planned to share her honeymoon with. Dana could have gotten married if she'd wanted to, but she wouldn't have been happy, and certainly not horny. To add to the insult, she probably would've tried everything possible not to get naked. What a mess she had gotten herself into again. It seemed she never quite got it right, at least not in the eyes of her family.

"Dana, come on." Jessie grabbed one of Dana's bags and slung it over her arm. "Isn't it gorgeous?"

"Gorgeous."

"Would a little enthusiasm kill you? You can either pout or you can relax and enjoy. It's not like you can get a refund for the trip. You agreed going to the Caribbean was a bad idea, and you didn't like any of the other options the travel agent said still had

3

openings and would take the vacation voucher."

"Did you want to go to the dude ranch?"

"Depends on the dudes I'd be riding, I mean ranching, with."

And there it was. Jessie only wanted a vacation lay. Why shouldn't she? Young, beautiful Jess had curves in all the right places. Dana had yet to meet a man whose cock didn't jump to attention at her friend's attributes. Jessie thought of this as a simple vacation. The previous night, at the last minute, Jessie had agreed to buy Frank's ticket and come with her. Jessie's job at the small Vermont newspaper could always wait another week. As she said, not much of interest happened from day to day anyway, and if her report on the school bake sale didn't go into the paper right away, no one would throw a fit.

Yet, for Dana, the trip was a necessary time for her to regroup. She had to discover who she was, what she wanted in life, and what it had to offer for the future. She had no job, having quit two weeks earlier in preparation for becoming Mrs. Frank Green. She had nowhere to live, having given up her apartment to move in with her future husband. At the end of the week, she had no real place to go, nowhere to call home.

"OMG." Jessie whistled and pointed toward a tall, muscular man dressed all in black. "The way the T-shirt grips those biceps makes me want to...."

Dana stared. How could she not? After all, he did fill out the shirt excessively well. Though there were other men surrounding the tall one, each buff and gorgeous in his own right, every one of them dressed in the same uniform. He stood apart. But the last thing she needed was to drool over a security guard at a resort. Her mother would have a conniption "He's an employee of the resort, Jess."

"I'm not suggesting you marry the man, but perhaps a good roll in the hay would do you some good. Don't be a snob."

"I am not a snob. I'm just not ready to jump into bed with other men. I only called off my wedding last night. I think I deserve a little time." Dana prayed she wasn't a snob, but could years of living under the same roof as her mother, Mrs. Nancy Stone, New

York socialite from Hell, have rubbed off? She hoped not.

Jessie rolled her eyes then strolled away. Maybe bringing her hadn't been such a good idea after all. She had the sensitivity of a goat, and Dana was pretty sure goats weren't at all sensitive to anything but their own urge to eat. Jessie's only sensitivity dealt with her urge for men. Dana's loud sigh stopped Jessie in her tracks, and she spun to face her.

"It's not like you wanted to marry Frank. In fact, you both agreed in front of three hundred of your parents' closest friends that you didn't want to get married. So why are you so glum? As far as I can see, you dodged a bullet."

"Just because someone knows they shouldn't be with someone doesn't make them mourn the loss any less," a tall, blond man with a voice soft as the wind said. He'd come from out of nowhere. He grabbed Dana's bag from Jessie's shoulder. "Come, Dana, and let's see what we can do to speed your healing."

"How did you know who I was?"

He shrugged. "Process of elimination, really. The

other guests have all made it up to the Haus. You two have not. Since one has a skip to her step, and the other is dragging, it doesn't take a mind reader to know which one of you called off a wedding."

"That obvious?"

"Only to someone empathetic. My name is Cemil Rowan, I'm part owner of the Wiccan Haus. Please"—he spread his hand and arm in the directions of the lobby door—"come in and let's get you situated. You appear tired, both emotionally and physically."

Dana decided not to question Cemil's assessment. Anyone could see she was about to fall where she stood. She hadn't slept in days, not since before she'd marched down the aisle, and certainly not last night. Her mind wandered to Frank. She hoped he'd fared better with his family than she had with hers.

"I'm sure your ex-fiancé is doing much the same as you are. He's mourning what should never have gone so far." Cemil gave her a kind smile. Before she could think on that one comment, Cemil diverted her attention to the exotic woman at the front desk. "This is Myron. She'll get you your keys. I'm sure I'll see you both at dinner"

Myron smiled. "Ms. Stone, we have your rooms ready."

"Rooms? I only ordered one room with two beds." Dana could afford only one room. Panicked, she reached into her bag to find the printout of her reservation.

"Relax, there's no extra charge for the second room." Myron smiled wider and pushed two keys toward her. "You'll find, at the Wiccan Haus, while you don't always get what you asked for, we strive to give you what you need."

Dana and Jessie were led by a random staff member to the farthest of three elevators and rode up to the third floor. The building seemed much larger inside than it had appeared on the outside. Walking down the long hallway, the bellhop grinned and opened a door to the left.

As Dana stepped inside, he shook his head. "This is Ms. Ranata's room. Yours is over here."

8

The breathtaking room calmed her inner being with its cream walls, bare of all art except a few dried branches arranged on the wall, and the aroma of herbs filling her nostrils, somehow easing her mood. The pale wood floors gleamed from the candles glowing throughout the room. A simple bed, cupboard, and chaise were the only other things occupying the space.

No clutter. No fuss. Only simplicity. Something she had never known. Her life had always been filled with many family members, family friends, parties, and huge, garish houses. She'd endured too much chaos and too much noise, had never thought or known what she truly needed might lie in simplicity, this lovely emptiness.

"Oh. I'm so sorry." A pixie-like woman with blonde, waist-length hair came out of the bathroom. "I'd meant to be long gone before you arrived." Laughing, she placed the dried herbs she held into a linen bag draped around her neck and across her chest. She scanned the room, assessing it, then wiped her hands on her long, flowing skirt. Her blue eyes twinkled, reminding Dana of Cemil.

"Yes. Cemil is my brother…and no, I don't have mind-reading ability." She reached out in greeting. "Everyone one who sees our sparkling blues puts two and two together. I'm Sage. It's a pleasure to meet you, Dana."

She took her proffered hand. "If the room isn't done, I can go to the lobby and read a book until it is."

"Don't be silly. I wanted to change a few items to make your stay better. I think I have the right soap and candles, but I had to work so quickly this time, I wasn't sure if the ingredients were strong enough." Sage shrugged, went to the door, and lit what appeared to be an enormous gray marijuana joint. After blowing the flame out, she fanned the spicy smoke over the door and through the room.

"What is that?" Dana asked. How odd that they would surround her room with what smelled like pot smoke.

"Oh, this?" Sage wafted the item around. "It's simply a smudge stick made of sage and a bit of sweet grass."

Dana still thought it looked like a doobie but didn't have the energy to prod any further.

Appearing satisfied, Sage said, "Yes. I think that does it."

"Does what?" Dana must have missed something. How did spreading smoke, no matter what kind it might be, around her doorway make any difference at all?

"Captures the essence of who you are, not what you have been or what your parents have molded you into becoming."

Her eyes burned with tears at the thought of her parents. They had declared, in front of all her wedding guests, that she was no longer a daughter of theirs. Well, her mother had said as much, but neither her sister, Ashlynn, nor father had argued the decree. A killing blow for Dana, who'd had to fight for every ounce of acceptance and love they had ever cared to dole out.

Sage floated out, and Dana decided not to question the sanity of the woman. She assumed

Wiccan meant white witch, but, for the first time, she wondered if perhaps the owners of Wiccan Haus truly believed they were witches, and not simply a tourist gag to get more people to come.

An increasing weariness came over her, and she wanted nothing more than to lie down. An escape from her life for a moment or two, escape the worry, guilt, fear, and regret she harbored deep inside.

***

Rekkus Duteigr entered the main office then quickly turned on his heel to walk right out. The Dark Ones, as most of the staff referred to Cyrus and Sarka Rowan, were at each other's throats again, and on the first day of a new week no less. Unlike Sage and Cemil, who never fought, it seemed to be all Sarka and Cyrus did. Two siblings who brought peace to everything they touched, two who brought chaos— the perfect yin and yang of family rivalry.

With the humans settled in for naps, thanks to the herbs Sage had left in their rooms, and the paranormals, or paras, arriving within the hour, he had a few minutes to relax until the portals opened and hell began anew. Or so he hoped.

Twice a day, the gateways to the paranormal world rumbled open, allowing those on the island to travel to many destinations around the world. They were the entrance to the Wiccan Haus for all para guests, as well. The portal at the Haus could be found down the hall from the offices in an obscure storage closet, while the other two randomly opened around the island. They were a security risk Rekkus was far from happy about dealing with. If he had his way, and that was only a matter of time, he would have all the portals but one closed.

"Where the hell do you think you're going?" Sarka's husky voice rumbled through him. Rekkus pivoted to meet her stare as she twisted her long black hair into a bun with a pencil. Great. Now he had to deal with her bad attitude. She always put her hair up when annoyed.

"Funny you should mention that. I'm trying to decide which hell I would rather deal with."

"Did you know the vamps were coming this week?" The hostility coming from Sarka was nearly tangible.

Rekkus let his head drop. Vampires, and Sarka's hatred for them, were not his favorite topics of conversation. Having no escape, he sat next to Cyrus. "Did you know, Cy?"

"No. Not that she believes me."

"You want me to believe no one in security knew we had a coven of vamps coming here this week and that neither Sage nor Cemil informed you?" Sarka asked.

"I have the complete guest list here." Rekkus tapped the clipboard he'd been carrying. "I also have Myron's tentative room assignments for every guest. Nowhere does it say *Race: vampire* on it. Sorry, luv."

It would seem Sage and Cemil—the Light Ones, as the staff called the blond siblings—had, in fact, left that information out. Though Rekkus hated to take sides in the silly family feud that erupted every week, Sarka's current argument had merit. Cemil should know when their bloodsucking guests made reservations. When vampires were on the property, a contingency plan had to be put into effect since willing hosts were required to feed them. At the moment, only two staff members fit that bill—not enough for the four vampires coming. And Hell could freeze over before Rekkus became vamp chow.

"Do you think that's an excuse?" Sarka folded her arms.

Cyrus threw his notepad on the desk separating him from his sister. "Sarka, for the love of the Goddess, do you honestly think we'd spring vamps on you like this for fun? I assure you, we would rather you do know. In fact, I'd rather bathe with piranhas than deal with you like this."

"You should know who the hell is in this building!"

"How? Neither of us is psychic."

Having had enough of the sibling squabble, Rekkus got to his feet. "If you'll excuse me, I'm going to take care of the dining issue."

"Wait for me," Cyrus said, following on his heels.

Once safely out of hearing range of Sarka, Rekkus mumbled, "Coward."

"You'd better believe it. The only person on this planet I'm scared of is my big sister."

"With good reason," Rekkus agreed.

Rekkus had been head of security at the Wiccan Haus since its doors opened five earlier, four years before the first human arrived on the island. About a year earlier, after taking a vacation of their own, the Light Ones had returned with the brilliant idea to offer the same services to the human race as they did to the paranormals—helping to heal and center those in need. Uncentered paras were more of a concern than humans since a para unable to control its powers stood as a danger to itself, others, and the secrecy of the *Para Pact*.

The Para Pact was a long-established agreement made between human governments and the para syndicate stating humans wouldn't hunt down shifters, vamps, and other mythical beings as long as the para world remained surreptitious and out of sight. Humans tend to panic when confronted with things that went bump in the night. Panic could lead to chaos, and chaos often led to lives being lost.

But humans were the ones Cemil and Sage most connected with. For them, Cemil worried. As an empath, he couldn't live knowing another person hurt. So the Light Ones had convinced Sarka it might work. They'd heal both humans and paras together, and, in Sage's rose-colored world, everyone would be happy friends. In truth, the arrangement had become a pain in Rekkus's ass. He had to worry about the effect paras had on humans, and what those humans did if they found out the true nature of the beasts they shared the same roof with.

In order for the arrangement to work, keeping the humans on a separate floor from the paras had been the first phase. The third elevator only stopped on the human floor. Sarka had transmuted the metal on the lift buttons so only a para's touch activated elevator two and only a human's the third.

If Rekkus wanted or needed to get to the human floor, he had to use a key. The human elevator wouldn't give him access any other way. The second phase they'd established had been in the dining hall to feed both races. Sage set herbs about the hall in an attempt to separate the two species, but, so far, they hadn't successfully managed it all of the time. Again, in Sage and Cemil's golden world, everyone got along. Combining the groups at meals and in classes seemed no big deal to them.

Rekkus and his staff worked in an eternal logistics nightmare. Their efforts to keep the two groups apart were a failure. Despite all the work security put into the separation, they still managed to find their way together. There appeared to be a great deal of coupling going on between the two groups every week as a result. But, thus far, nobody had returned to the mainland with stories of ghoulies and ghosties and long-legged beasties. As long as no one told tales about the place, Sarka wasn't coming down on him, and Rekkus didn't care who fucked whom.

"Was there a reason you were looking for me, Rekkus?" Cyrus asked.

"Yeah, actually, but had I known Sarka was in there, I wouldn't have come within a mile of that room."

"What is it?" As if anticipating the reason, Cyrus removed the glove from his right hand and held it out, palm-side up.

"You don't have to use your gift."

Cyrus cranked his head to the left until his neck cracked. "You wouldn't give me something if you felt it could harm me. Besides, using my powers every now and then is therapeutic, or so Sage keeps telling me."

Rekkus tossed him the antique wristwatch he'd found on the path leading from the docks. Cyrus took it held it for a brief second then handed it back. "It belongs to Dana Stone. She recently called off her wedding and came from a—"

"Really, Cyrus, the name is all I required. I don't give a bloody damn about the human's issues."

"You use me as a lost-and-fucking-found, you get the information I get."

Rekkus chuckled and waved him away. Of all the siblings, Cyrus was the least happy with his gift. As a retrocog, he had the ability to see things about the

19

owner of an object that not even he wanted to know. His powers were what had originally caused the siblings to open the healing resort. He'd spent too many years reading items to find out who killed whom, who stole what, and who cheated on whom. From the age of thirteen, when his powers had come to the notice of the Para Syndicate, Cyrus had been in demand. By twenty-one, he'd been famous. Every para knew his name. By twenty-seven, he'd been a wreck.

Cyrus had been unable to sleep or eat, the memories in his head haunting him. Every murder played in his mind's eye when he held a murder weapon. Every wrong deed came to life as if he lived it, whenever he read an object. He'd started wearing gloves so only the items he needed to focus on would enter his brain, but that made it worse. Now the only items he tended to touch were evil ones. He no longer got to retrieve a baby's blanket when it dropped to the floor, to feel the mother's love and the child's happiness. His world had become dark and morbid.

The Syndicate had hired Rekkus as his personal

bodyguard when it became obvious not everyone liked Cyrus's gift. Strange accidents began to happen at an ever-growing and alarming rate. One night, a group of rogue paras attacked and killed members of the coven in retribution for information Cyrus had given to the Syndicate. Cyrus's three middle sisters had been amongst the dead. Rekkus, by making a split-second decision not to allow the four remaining siblings to get out of the car that fateful night, had saved their lives.

After that, Cyrus shut down.

Nothing and no one could get him to open up. So, when the Syndicate offered him the island as compensation, the siblings took it with all four sets of hands. Not only would it allow for the healing, but also allowed them to mourn the deaths of their three sisters. To ensure the safety of his remaining family Cyrus begged Rekkus to come and be their head of security. Unable to deny his friend the one lifeline to sanity he had left, Rekkus agreed.

While Rekkus secured the island, using every magical ability at his disposal through the Syndicate, the three siblings spent the following year focused on healing Cyrus. At the end of it, Cyrus suggested they do the same for others. Now, as long as he kept his hands gloved, he lived a relatively normal life. But threats still remained, and Rekkus's job to keep the four safe and secure from the factions still intent on revenge hadn't changed.

Having been Cyrus's best friend since they'd ridden tricycles, Rekkus hadn't seen him this comfortable or at ease since their early teens. Only that knowledge kept Rekkus on the island taking care of silly humans and weak paras—paras he secretly thought unworthy of the name since they needed a spa, but if Cyrus found peace by helping them, who was Rekkus to argue?

Approaching the front desk, Myron glanced at him from the playing cards she'd spread out on the desk. "Room seven."

"Not my room. The room for—"

"Room seven for Ms. Stone." She lifted a seven of hearts so he could see it.

Rekkus nodded, headed to the elevator, inserted

the key, and rode to the third floor. With any luck, Dana Stone would not be napping yet. They still had forty-five minutes until the portal opened, and that meant the herbs hadn't fully infused the room. He hated drugging the humans to get the paras on the island, but its boom rattled the building and the noise could wake the dead. So, better to get the humans in their rooms and resting before sunset. Unfortunately, that only happened at certain times. Although he had tried again and again to work out the timing, they never were able to get the ferry to arrive after it opened and still have time to get everyone checked in.

Arriving at the room at the end of the hall, he knocked gently. If she slept, he would leave the piece of jewelry on the doorknob. About to give up when there was no answer, he started to place the jewelry on the knob when the door cracked a bit to reveal a bleary-eyed, disheveled woman, whose skin had to be the softest he had ever seen and called to him to touch it. His inner animal roared to life, and Rekkus reared back like he'd been hit square in the solar plexus. She seemed small compared to his six foot five frame.

23

And every inch of him wanted to take her curvaceous body hard and fast and make her his.

"Can I help you?" She lifted a hand to stifle a yawn.

Centering himself to control his beast, he focused on the item he held. "Sorry to disturb you, Ms. Stone, but I found your watch on the path coming from the ferry. I wanted to return it to you."

She stared at it, confused, taking it from him. Her fingers barely grazed his hand, but the contact burned. "Thank you. I don't know how I could have lost it."

Unable to say anything after her brief touch, Rekkus nodded in what had to make him appear a complete moron.

For a moment, her dark-chocolate colored eyes met his, and his breath hitched.

"Thank you. My grandmother willed this to me, and it's very special. I don't know how I can repay you."

Fuck me. Focusing on her lips, he wondered if they were as soft as they seemed and how they would feel on his body.

24

"Excuse me?" Clearly offended at what he'd evidently muttered aloud and not waiting for him to say anything more, she closed the door, leaving him standing and staring at the brass seven room number.

"'Fuck me?'" He groaned. "Rekkus, you are a right idiot."

Not only had he said the words aloud, but had a sneaking suspicion he hadn't come across that watch by accident. He also suspected it wasn't simply what it appeared. He couldn't put his finger on it, but something in the timepiece hummed with magic. And he'd long ago stopped believing in happenstance.

Walking down the hall, he let out a growl loud enough to shake the pictures on the beautifully decorated walls.

Damn the Fates.

Chapter Two

Dana ate her meal in silence. Though the food tasted fantastic, she didn't have much of an appetite, and she doubted anyone would notice her push the entree around the plate. Jessie, who had come to get her for dinner, ate as if it were her last meal, savoring every bite, and when servers asked if she would like more, she jumped on it.

The image of the hotel employee who had come to Dana's door crept to the front of her mind. His chiseled face, Anglican nose, and the rough stubble on his face, evidence he'd shaved much earlier that morning, burned into her brain. Dana might be tall at five foot nine, but he'd made her feel petite. And he'd wanted to eat her alive, or *fuck her*, as he'd so eloquently put it. She might no longer be engaged, but guilt and heat filled her for the attraction she had for the barbaric man.

Smiling at the right times in the conversation, Dana managed to answer the questions of a sweet, older couple from Pennsylvania. She really would have been happier to eat in her room, but the rules stated every member must be in the dining room for dinner. Sage had mentioned something about head counts to ensure no guests wandered the island or got lost after dark. Since tall, dark, and blunt wasn't in the room, it seemed the staff was exempt from the *everyone eats dinner* rule.

Jessie followed Dana's gaze as she looked to the entrance of the dining hall yet again. "What are you looking for?"

"No one—I mean nothing."

Glancing away, Dana checked out the printed list of the evening's activities left in the center of the table. She wished heading to bed and pulling the covers over her head was one of the choices.

Wondering how much time she had before the activities began, she checked her watch and noticed it gone. Panicked, she excused herself and left the room. She'd lost her grandmother's antique silver watch *again*. She'd have to retrace her steps and hope against hope it had fallen off in her room. Vowing to get the clasp fixed as soon as they returned to the mainland, she thought it bizarre that the timepiece, which hadn't left her wrist in three years except when she removed it to shower or swim or bathe, had managed to fall off unnoticed twice in one day.

As she approached the elevators, Dana yelled for the person entering one of them to hold it for her. Running the last few feet, she thanked the beautiful, dark-haired woman and headed to the rear of the car, keeping her ass to the wall. The two other passengers had skin the color of porcelain and exuded sexuality from every pore. The woman slid next to her—damn, even her movements were sensual—too close for Dana's comfort and licked her blood-red lips. Dana edged closer to the walls. The car stopped. Dana tried to move, but for a second her feet seemed glued to the floor. Two sets of dark eyes pierced her soul, and her blood raced. The man exuded hunger. The kind of hunger Dana had when she forgot to eat breakfast. Finally, the doors parted with a long, loud ding, far louder than she'd remembered the first time she'd ridden it.

Without looking over her shoulder, she tried not to run down the hall to the last door on the left. Fumbling with her key, she was slightly surprised yet thankful to find she hadn't locked the door. Opening it, she slipped inside and twisted the lock behind her to avoid the two intimidating people who followed her. An energizing mix of adrenalin and fear pumped through her—never had she been so scared.

After taking a moment to call herself a fool in every way possible, she searched for the missing watch. Much to her dismay, it seemed to have vanished. On all fours, she checked under the bed, now remade and appearing as if she had never taken a nap on it. After checking under the wardrobe in the corner of the room, she rose, about to enter the bathroom when its door opened. All six foot plus of the man who had returned her watch earlier stood naked, obviously having just gotten out of the shower. Her shower. And what the hell was he doing naked in her room?

Surprise lit his golden eyes. Heat rose between them. Before Dana could ask why he'd chosen her bathroom to wash in, let alone for an explanation of his nakedness, he lifted her into his arms, pinned her against the wall, and his mouth descended on hers. Her brain shut off. He said something that sounded like, *you felt it too*, but the buzzing in her ears drowned every thought but the feel of his body and lips against hers.

Too shocked to fight at first, she finally collected her wits and pulled away. But when she began to question him, his lips captured the words and nothing else seemed possible except to let them. No thoughts, no actions made any difference, only her need to kiss him back. His tongue dove deep, waltzing with hers and demanding she meet his movements.

Damn! This man can kiss!

His hands cupped her buttocks, pressing her into intimate contact with his hard, impressive cock. She ground her hips against him, wanting nothing more than to remove the barrier of clothing between them.

She gripped his bare back, first for support then to prevent him from moving away. Nibbling his way down her neck, he pushed her loose-knit blouse to the side, giving him more access to her sensitive flesh. As he worked his way over her collarbone to her shoulder, some semblance of sanity resumed. Other than their brief meeting earlier, Dana had no idea who this naked, admittedly drop-dead-gorgeous stranger was. Only that he'd almost ravished her. The man, who hadn't even grunted when he'd lifted her against the wall, could probably take her right there without her consent. Panic crept in.

"Stop!" She shoved him with all the strength she could muster. His head shot up, his eyes filled with confusion and passion. "Put me down. Now!" Without pause, he lowered her, inch by tantalizing inch, until her toes finally reached the floor.

"Better?"

"That can't happen. Not again." She stumbled away, bumping into the table, nearly knocking over the candle that sat upon it. "What are you doing in my room?"

"Your room?" he asked in a voice still deep with passion. For the first time, she noticed the hint of an accent, Scottish, maybe British. He turned away, giving her the perfect view of his ass and the most gorgeous tribal tattoo of a tiger on his shoulder. Entering the bathroom, he grabbed one of the folded towels, and she diverted her scrutiny to give him time to cover his muscular hips. A sense of relief washed over her. Although he could have overpowered her, he hadn't. In fact, even as aroused as he was, he'd been gentle and complied with her demand.

"Why do you think this is your room?"

"Of course this is my room. How did you get in, and why are you taking a shower in here?" To her own ears, she sounded shrewish. "Don't you have your own room in the servant's quarters?" She cringed as her mother's pompous attitude slipped from her lips.

"I am no one's servant," he growled. "And I have a room, and you, lady, are standing in it."

"I'm not sharing a room with you."

"I didn't ask you to." He strode to the wardrobe, threw open the door, and pulled out a pair of jeans and a T-shirt. "As you can see, this is my stuff, my clothes. This is my room."

"But I don't understand. I thought…. Oh, no. I am so sorry, but this room resembles mine, and it's at the end of the hall." Dana stumbled toward the door, hit the edge of the coffee table, and cursed as the corner scraped her leg. She'd sport a bruise in the morning.

"Careful."

"Sorry, I really…I'll just leave you—"

"What lift did you get into?"

"What?"

"Lift, elevator, the thing that brought you to this floor?"

"I don't know. The second, maybe. Someone held it for me when I got there." Heat crept to the roots of her hair. She had made a colossal ass of herself. No wonder the man had come on to her with such force. He must have thought she'd searched him out in order to get laid. "I'm so sorry. I'll just let myself out."

"No," he barked, but then his features softened. "No. I'll escort you back to your room. Let me get dressed first. Don't go out into the hallway without me."

"I'm sure I'll be safer out there than in here with you." She doubted she'd ever be able to forget the image of him sliding the pants over his firm ass. Or that he went commando to boot.

Another growl, this time deep-laced with so much frustration and need that, had she not been so keen to exit the room, she might have laughed. "I'm simply worried about you causing a riot."

A riot? "Fine, if you really feel like you have to escort me, you can take me to the dining hall. I'm sure my friend is wondering where I am." An outright lie. The only thing Jessie currently worried about? Whose bed to share for that week, but Mr. Buff-Muscles didn't need to know that.

Dana took a deep breath in, smelling him as he walked by...like sex on very firm, muscular legs. Her only disappointment—she hadn't seen more of his ass. She'd bet that would have been a picture to keep her hot on any winter night.

"After you, Ms. Stone." Finished dressing, he opened the locked door, turned, raised an eyebrow, and waited for her to exit before closing it behind them.

She noticed he hadn't locked the door this time either, but then doing so might impede his secret liaisons. "You should probably lock your door when you leave."

"Don't need to."

Of course not. Who would dare to enter his room when he wasn't there? She made a face at him when he passed her. He might be sexy as hell, lick-him-like-a-lollipop sexy, but he seemed too sure of himself for her.

He jabbed the button with such force, she was sure it almost cracked under the pressure.

"I'm sorry for the mix-up and leading you to believe I came there for something else."

"Don't ever apologize to me. I was out of line. The fault is completely mine."

"I won't tell anyone. I don't want to put your job in jeopardy."

"*My job* was never what was in jeopardy, Ms. Stone."

He entered the car and waited for her to follow when a short red-headed man and gorgeous blonde woman, whose barely-there dress left very little to the imagination, tried to get in with them. He stood in the entrance, blocking their entry. "Take the next one, Max."

"Oh, come on, Rekkus. There is more than enough room." The stupid man either ignored the tension her tall security guard broadcasted in his direction or didn't care.

"I said, take the next one."

Lifting both hands in surrender, Max stepped away. "Serena and I will take the next one."

When the doors closed on their shocked faces, Dana said, "They could have come with us."

"No."

The ride seemed to take forever. As she stared at his ass, she wondered what it would have been like to let him take her against that wall in his room. What if she hadn't stopped him? What if...?

Shaking her head, she focused on something else. "What kind of name is Rekkus?"

"Welsh."

"Oh."

He took a deep breath, filling his broad chest until she wanted to run her hands under his shirt to feel it again. As the doors parted, he stood in the entrance, preventing her from leaving. "It's a family name. We are Welsh."

"Okay."

"Um, Rekkus, are you going to stand in there all day, or are you going to let others use it?"

Dana glanced around him to see Sage holding another basket of dried weeds.

"Oh, hello, Ms. Stone. Whatever are you doing in *this* elevator?"

"I got on the wrong one by mistake."

"Oh dear. Well, good thing you ran into Rekkus here. You'll be in good hands."

You have no idea. "Yes, thank you."

"Rekkus, did you just growl at me?" Sage pushed him out of the way, as if he were a toddler not listening to a parent, and shooed Dana out. "Really, growling at me. As if. Rekkus, make sure you take

Dana to the meditation room. That's where she should be tonight."

"As you wish." He bent over in a mock bow and placed his hand on Dana's lower back, sending tingles all the way up her spine. "You heard the lady. Meditation room for you." They walked the rest of the way in silence, but he bristled over what she could not say.

"You said something about feeling it, too, earlier when we, well, you…. I mean us," Dana said.

He turned her toward him, his golden eyes searching her face as if to memorize it. "It would be best, I think, if you forgot anything I said and that you ever met me."

"But—"

"This is the meditation room. I'm sure they will be able to help you relax again. Enjoy your stay and please remember, for your own safety, you are only to take the third elevator."

Before Dana had the opportunity to call after him, he retreated down the beige hallway, reminding her of a caged animal at the zoo. Shaking that thought, but not the images of him naked, from her brain, she entered the mediation room.

There were things about this place that didn't make sense and, quite frankly, Dana felt too drained to try to figure them out. She'd come there to heal, not to get laid. And though she feared saying no to Rekkus might be a mistake that would haunt her later on, right now, finding peace with herself had to come first. He would only muddy things up.

Even as she thought it, she didn't really believe that.

Chapter Three

Rekkus stomped into the office, not caring that three sets of eyes stared at him with icy-blue crispness. "I'm going for a swim."

"Now? There are still guests roaming the grounds," Sarka said. "You can't yet. You must wait until the humans are in bed, at least."

"Now. And I'll be discreet, as I always am."

"We also have to deal with the diet issues for the vamps."

"You know what? Let the kitchen deal with it. I don't give a shit." About to leave, he stopped when Cemil made one of those annoying noises he made when he found something interesting. "What?"

"No matter how hard you run tonight, you can't run from your destiny."

"I'm not running from anything."

"Did he just growl at Cemil?" Sarka asked.

"He did." Cyrus put down the paper he'd been reading to watch his friend.

A twinkle lit Sarka's eyes. "Interesting."

"Sage just called here and said he growled at her in the elevator, too." Cyrus added.

"Really." Sarka pulled the pen out of her hair, shook her black locks then tapped the pen against her chin.

"I am right-fucking-here, you prats," Rekkus said between clenched teeth.

Cemil, who'd remained quiet during his siblings' exchange, closed his lids and grabbed Rekkus's arm. With a gasp, he dropped it. "His mate is on the island."

"What?" Sarka and Cyrus asked.

Rekkus sneered. "She is *not* my mate."

"Who?" the Dark Ones asked again.

If they thought he had growled before, they hadn't heard anything yet. "Cemil...."

Sarka, obviously enjoying his discomfort, smirked. "I didn't think one could growl out the name 'Cemil.'"

"Neither did I, Sarka, but he did." Cyrus furrowed his brow, staring at his friend with great interest.

"Swim. Gonna. Go. Swim. In case I feel compelled to do something to all three of you I might *not* regret in the morning." He turned on Cemil as he got up. "Don't say another fucking word."

He'd barely crossed the threshold of her office when Sarka asked, "So, you think one of us should go after him?"

"Not on your life." Cyrus said.

As he walked out the door past Myron, who'd laid a playing card on the reception desk, Rekkus stopped and cover the cards with his palm and demanded, "Why did you put Dana Stone in the room you did?"

She focused on the card she held for another second before meeting his gaze, not intimidated in the least. "I ran the numbers when she made the initial reservation. Room six came up, but, for some reason, when I saw her coming along the path this afternoon, I sensed I should run the numbers again, and that time a seven came up. So I pinged Sage and asked her to change the rooms."

Rekkus didn't want to hear that. He wanted to hear it had been a coincidence, that the room they'd assigned her had been the last one available, or that someone else didn't like it so she'd volunteered to take it. He did not want to hear the numbers, which in an indirect way meant the Fates wanted her in the mirror-image of his room. The Fates had placed her there so when she made the mistake of getting on the wrong elevator, it would never occur to her she might not be in her room until it was too late.

He had six days to get through till she left the island. Then his life might return to normal. Six days to hold off this driving lust to take the beautiful, voluptuous woman in his arms and fuck her until she begged him never to stop. Worse, he had six days in which to ignore Dana's presence, knowing even then his life would never be the same.

Running out the front door, he ignored everyone, even the vampire leering at a strolling human couple who came too close, and headed directly for the wooded area near the Haus. His shoes were the first to come off, followed by his shirt, discarded and left to fall where it landed. He stripped off his pants and kicked them to the side, where they caught on a bush. Once naked, he looked to the moon, not completely full, but full enough to increase his powers. He growled one last time and allowed the shift to take him. From full human to black tiger, the largest of were-cats. And the last of his kind, last of the great black tiger streak. Only his golden eyes remained to show any resemblance to his human likeness.

His massive paws crushed the dead leaves underfoot as Rekkus raced through the forest, pushing his body, allowing the animal within to release the pent-up rage and frustration. The Fates were not simply cruel, they had a diabolical sense of humor. Not only had they left him alone as the sole remaining Duteigr, but when they finally did send him someone, his mate turned out to be human. Not one ounce of para blood ran through her veins.

Having run to an area of the lakeshore he knew few humans hiked to, at least at night, Rekkus paused. He let out a loud hiss of frustration and paced along the water's edge. Unless he left the island, avoiding

Dana seemed nearly impossible. Damned if he knew how to avoid her. He needed her gone. He didn't have any use for a mate and didn't want one, least of all a weak human. Convinced with enough willpower it might be possible to control the problem, he dove into the water. Coming up for air, he shifted to his human side and strolled out of the lake. As he retraced his steps to find the clothes he'd stripped out of, he wished, not for the first time, he had followed through on his plan and left a box of clothes nearby.

"I was searching for you," Serena, the woman from the elevator, approached, holding his pants with one finger.

"Serena," he greeted, relieved to be free of the lake. No one who knew Serena voluntarily got in the water with her. At least no one with an ounce of brains, and he wasn't stupid. The siren went from seductress to killer in a second. In the middle of her second consecutive week at the resort, she had found his clothes before he had again. She already knew too much about his behavior for his sense of security.

"I so love coming across your pants and knowing

you aren't in them." She inched closer, allowing her breasts to press against his wet chest. Her lips brushed his collarbone, and she reached down to cup his cock.

He wondered why she, a woman designed to seduce men, left him unaffected now, when, only a few days ago, she'd made him hard and alleviated his desires.

Grabbing her by the shoulders, he pushed her away. "Sing, Siren."

"Excuse me?"

"Sing."

"But you made me sign a pact that stated I would sing for no one."

"I'm allowing you to sing now, for me, to entice me."

Serena cocked her head at Rekkus as if he'd lost his marbles. And maybe he had. "Very well."

She took a step so her feet touched the water. The pool shimmered with life, as she did. Her eyes, normally a brilliant blue, churned with the colors of the oceans. Licking her lips, she opened her mouth and sang.

Come, men of the land,

Come and meet me on the strand.

Your hearts they've grown weary, and my eyes are all teary,

For the man I need is away on the sea.

Come, men of the land,

Come walk in the sand.

Your soul is now mine, and like the fish on your line,

The man that I need is now one with the sea.

Rekkus listened to her voice, so pure it had dragged men to their deaths in the murky depths of the sea. The same voice had made him hard with want and lust when he'd caught her bathing naked at the hot spring on the other end of the island. Yet, here she stood, willing to give him a sexual escape that would leave most paras sated and most humans dead, yet he felt nothing. Not a twinge of interest left in him for her. The only image in his mind was of Dana and her soft curves.

Damn the Fates to Hell.

"So, it's true what they're saying?" Serena

47

touched his bare shoulder in a soft gesture of support. "Only a man who has found his mate, no matter para or human, could resist my song."

"But *she* is human."

"So? You can spend all of your time fighting it, or you can give into what, from all I have heard, is beautiful and wondrous. But your time is ticking. You only have six days to convince her to stay because, once she's off the island, you'll have a hard time courting her long-distance. And everyone knows you'll never leave here, not so long as there is any threat to Cyrus."

"It's better if she leaves. She isn't our kind."

"Think on this, Rekkus—once she leaves and you relinquish any hold on her, there will be a long line of paras who will go after her. There has to be something in her for the Fates to give the black tiger prince a human princess."

The siren went to sing again, but Rekkus placed a silencing finger on her lips. "The pact is reinstated, no singing."

She shrugged, throwing the pants at him before

diving into the deepest part of the lake and disappearing with a splash of her beautiful, shimmering tail.

Chapter Four

Meditation, though nice, did nothing to release her frustration. The hot herbal bath relaxed her but still didn't get to the root of the issue. Dana was horny as hell, and she blamed the hot security guy. She wanted him with a fever she'd never experienced and had woken twice in the middle of the night, sweat pouring off her, cursing the erotic dreams haunting her.

If her plans to reunite with her family when she got home were going to happen, she needed to make sure she didn't return involved with a security guard. Her mother, never one to treat someone she considered a blue-collar worker kindly in the best of situations, would see this as yet another act of defiance from Dana and follow through with the threat to disown her. Unfortunately, Dana's hormones didn't seem to give a damn what her head told them.

Now, after a shower and a quick in-room breakfast of grapefruit and granola, Dana decided what she had to do. To get on with the healing, she had to get rid of her desire for Rekkus. She'd take a page from Jessie's book and go for it. She'd enjoy the moment, enjoy the man, and when she left, she'd have a great memory of an unforgettable evening. A secret liaison only she knew about.

Except her. She'd remember it for the rest of her life.

Unfortunately, following through with her plan proved harder to put into action than she'd expected. For one, Rekkus was MIA. And, although the second elevator took her to his floor, hers didn't, and now the that lift wouldn't work for her. She pushed the button and nothing happened. After camping out in front of the elevator for two hours hoping someone needed it, she finally gave up. It appeared the other floor liked to sleep in.

Myron at the front desk offered no help. She said the numbers weren't in Dana's favor, whatever that meant. So, Dana wandered the island in hopes of finding him out and about. No luck. She followed the stone path to the Haus, way past lunch and close to dinner, deflated and still as horny as previously, only now her stomach protested the lack of food on top of everything else.

When she entered the lobby, Myron shook her head before any questions even left her lips. Finally, Dana accepted the inevitable—Rekkus didn't want to be found, and she was starving by that time. The rumbling in her stomach far outweighed the ache at the apex of her thighs. She had almost finished her salad when Jessie strolled in with a satisfied glow about her.

"Isn't this place fantastic? I had the most wonderful massage and mud soak." Jessie threw herself into the vacant seat across from Dana and frowned. "You don't look so good. Didn't you get any sleep last night?"

Dana wanted to punch her. "No, not really."

"You might think about asking that Sage chick if she can give you something to help you rest. I mean, you went days working up to the wedding not sleeping then you didn't sleep at all the night of, and now last night, either."

Dana shrugged. She wasn't about to tell Jessie she couldn't sleep because she obsessed about the hot hotel employee they'd seen as they'd gotten off the boat, and then later she'd almost let fuck her brains out without even knowing his name. And she'd never admit she'd pushed him away and told him to stop.

Dana shrugged again. "I'm sure tonight will be better."

"If you say so. By the way, did you find your watch?"

Perplexed, Dana considered her friend for a moment and then she remembered the whole reason she had gone to the room the previous night had been to look for the watch.

"No, I've no idea where it is. I've had the thing for years and now I've lost it not once, but twice in a day."

"I'm sure it'll turn up. Maybe you should talk to the woman at the front desk. You know, the one always playing cards. Can you imagine playing solitaire all day long? I wandered by this morning and the owners were there. They didn't say a word. If I

53

did that at work, I'd be fired so quick. We go days where there is nothing at all to report, but I'd still get let go."

Dana tuned out whatever else she might have said; Jessie had a way of going on about things as if her life was so very hard. Born with silver spoons in their mouths, neither Jessie nor Dana had suffered a hard life at all. And Dana was in such a mood, she might say something nasty about how Jessie wasn't likely to lose her job since Daddy had bought the paper to allow her to have a job somewhere writing when no one else hired her. But then Dana had been able to jump into a PR job straight out of college because the owner knew her father, too. Pot calling the kettle black? Maybe a little.

A sudden chill sliced down her spine. All eyes seemed locked on her from across the dining room, with people whispering as they came in.

"Are you even listening to me, Dana?"

"Sorry."

"What are you so focused on?" Jessie twisted her head around and frowned. "Why are they all staring at you as if you're a freak at a carnival?"

"Geez, thanks, Jess."

"Sorry, but they are. And have you noticed only the pretty people, and I mean the ultra-perfect people, sit over on that side of the dining hall? I noticed it at lunch. Something strange is going on here."

"Yes, Jessie. It's a conspiracy against the average people."

"Did you do something today to make them all stare like that? You know, falling in the hallway, spilling something on one of their pristine beings?"

"No, I've no idea. And now I'm getting creeped out by the attention. I think I'll head out and find Sage. Maybe you're right. I just need some sleep." Dana bid her friend good-bye, grabbed the plum off her plate, and strolled through the wandering corridors to the front desk. Sitting there, as always, Myron played what did appear to be solitaire.

"Hi, Myron," Dana said, glancing at the name badge that read *Celeste*. "Oh, sorry. I thought your name was Myron."

"It is. I seem to lose my real tag all the time, so I

took Celeste's." She picked up her cards and laid them in a fashion unfamiliar to Dana. *Maybe not solitaire.* "Whatever you are looking for is at the lake southwest of here. Follow the path and walk about ten minutes. You can't miss it."

"I didn't tell you I lost anything." Of course, how many times could she lose a watch before staff started to think she was a complete twit with a brain the size of a T. Rex.

"You didn't have to. Your numbers told me where you're supposed to be. You must hurry if you want to make it in time."

Baffled by the flaky lady behind the counter, Dana didn't budge. She studied the cards—the king of hearts over the queen of spades, next to a seven of diamonds, and a card facing down and to the side. *Really? That says "Go to the lake and you'll find your watch?"*

So maybe this nutty group really did believe in magic after all. To each their own.

Myron gathered the cards and stacked them. "You must hurry."

"So you said." Shaking her head, Dana forged out of the lobby and into the cool New England—at least she assumed they were still in New England—air. Though a big part of her wanted to take her damned time walking the path, the small part said, *What if crazy card-lady is right. What if...?*

Shaking off the thought, Dana strolled the path. She hadn't remembered it being so far to the lake and, as the trail took a hard right, a black-and-gray beast came into view, swimming in the water. Tiger-like, both in size and stripes, but couldn't be, impossible, and how the hell had a tiger gotten on this island?

Hiding behind a tree, she closed her eyes and focused on calming down so whatever the thing was didn't hear her. She gazed at the sky and braced herself as she peeked around the spruce. Should the animal be looking the other way, she'd make a run for the Haus and get help. If it saw her, she'd play dead. Supposedly, that worked for bears, but she'd never been in a situation requiring her to know what to do with a tiger. Perhaps the lack of sleep and stress was playing havoc on her senses. Maybe, just maybe, she was imagining it all. Taking another stabilizing breath, she snuck a look. There, in all his naked glory, stood Rekkus. Naked, wet, and hard. Oh, so very hard.

Again!

Holy hell. Hiding again, she tried to settle her raging hormones. Not only was she losing her mind by seeing beasts that obviously weren't there, but, now, she couldn't compose herself and she feared she'd jump his bones the minute he spotted her. After spending all day searching for him, her courage failed her when she succeeded.

She stepped away from the tree to face her desire. A stick beneath her foot cracked, and Rekkus's head snapped up. The hunger in his eyes nearly caused her to run in the other direction.. No man had ever looked at her with such lust.

Instead of the heady rush she'd assumed she'd feel, the one all the romance novels she'd read said the heroine experienced, a severe case of nerves attacked. Why was he looking at her that way? And he *obviously* wanted her.

Aware of her beauty, Dana also acknowledged her full figure. Although she had great curves that drew men to her, she was still a good size eighteen. However, what was it about her that had this god-like man considering her with such blatant desire and longing? Encouraged, she made her way down the path, stopping at the sandy beach.

"Did you see a tiger?" *Really, Dana, what the fuck kind of opening was that?*

"A tiger? Here? In Maine?" He shook his head and continued to pace in the shallow water, running a hand through his hair in a show of frustration. Just as her nerves stretched nearly to their breaking point, he asked, "Why are you here?"

"Myron told me to come to the lake." She took a few steps toward him.

He stopped, glared in the Myron's direction at the Haus then began to pace again. "Damn her. I spend all day avoiding you and she sends you right to me. You must leave now."

"Why?"

"It's not safe for you here with me. I left you

59

alone last night, but, if you stay, I'm not sure I can honor a request to stop a second time."

"I felt it, too," she blurted, unable to keep it to herself any longer.

Rekkus moved so fast, she never saw him actually take a step. Strong, wet arms wrapped around her, and her breasts pressed against his chest. His eyes searched hers. He must have seen what he searched for because his lips were on hers with feverous desire before she formed another thought, demanding she open for him. And no part of her considered denying him anything. Butterflies churned in her stomach until she shook. In all the years with Frank, and it had been a great many, she'd never felt this, like fire threatened to engulf her.

Dana wound her arms around his neck, running her fingers through his damp hair and deepening the kiss. His moan allowed her to gather the nerve and strength to urge him forward. He forced her past her comfort zone into accepting the sexy seductress screaming to be let out. She knew what he most desired because she wanted it too. Wanted him, all of him, every naked inch, right there, next to the lake, not even a ten-minute walk from the Haus. Anyone might stumble across them, and she didn't care. It almost added to the allure of having him. What she needed it to be.

Dana pulled away from the kiss. She wanted to see what she touched, witness the effect she had on him. Not an ounce of fat graced his body, but his muscles contracted beautifully under her caresses. As she reached his stomach and descended lower, his breath hitched, and her eyes locked on his. She fisted his cock, and he hissed, throwing his head back. Soaking in his magnificence displayed under the glow of the full moon, she slid her palm over the head of his cock. It jerked, and wet droplets formed on the tip. She brought her fingers to her lips to taste him, to savor his essence before returning her attention to his hard-on. Transfixed, she watched her hand work the length. A tingling at the base of her neck forced her to look up. Face tense, he held something back, as if unsure. Perhaps out of care for her, or worry his eagerness might scare her off? But how could she know in the heat of the moment, and with no time to think on it?

Rekkus's heady, woody scent, mixed with citrus, filled her senses, his kiss awe-inspiring until her brain clouded. He traced fingers over her clothes, as though annoyed she still had any on, and she frantically worked the shorts down her hips, kicking them to the side, her underwear soon following. Grabbing her ass, he lifted her so she straddled his hips then he walked into the lake until their bodies were half-submerged. He gripped her hips, pressing her against his erection.

Leaning away, he growled, "You have to be very sure about this. Once we do this, there is no going back."

"I'm sure."

"I don't think I can stop again if you don't put an end to this now."

Stop? Why the hell would she want him to stop? She ached for his cock, actually believed if he didn't make love her to her, she'd catch fire. "I don't care."

"You must because, once we go through this, I won't be able to let you go."

"I just want to be with you," she practically begged while kissing her way up his neck to the soft spot below his ear, hoping that would shut him up. She didn't want to talk or think—only experience him. He rewarded her with a purr. Smiling, she moved her hips enough to bring the tip of his cock to her entrance. "I need you."

"Dana, if we mate tonight, I—"

"Mate, fuck, make love, I don't care. Please...." She anchored him between her thighs. Finally, all those years of horseback-riding lessons had paid off. She leaned into the security of his arms within the water then pushed against him, using her heels against his buttocks as leverage until he'd impaled himself fully inside her.

"Yes!" *Finally*. She clenched around him as if fearing he'd withdraw from her.

Neither Rekkus or she moved. Only their eyes met. For the rest of her life, his image would be burned in her mind.

He stayed firmly inside her but allowed her to float. His stare never left her as the cool water washed over her breasts and stomach still confined within her blouse.

One hand fastened onto her hip while he spread the fingers of the other over her soft belly and up to her breasts. He rubbed a rough palm over her hardened nipples one at a time, before lightly pinching each through the fabric. Releasing her hip, he reached behind her, gripping her shoulders, drawing her against him, forcing him deeper still. His gaze raked up her figure, resting on her chest. She glanced down to find her dark nipples clearly visible through her wet cotton blouse.

She wrapped an arm around his shoulder, clutching his ass with the other. Holding on with her thighs, she rode him as if afraid he'd buck her off. He met each of her thrusts, slowly at first, then picked up the rhythm. Within the space of a few moments, his animal urges took over, and he ravaged her like nothing she'd ever experienced. Every long stroke filled Dana until she thought she couldn't take much more.

She arched. The first quakes of orgasm began,

yet she fought to keep them at bay, wanting their joining to last. But when Rekkus dragged her back to him, forcing full contact again, she fought no more.

His lips covered hers, catching her scream of pleasure. As his own orgasm raked through him, she rode it out with him, every shudder sending a stronger one through her until she no longer knew where her orgasm ended and his began.

When the mutual shaking had gradually subsided, she opened her eyes. He hugged her close for what seemed like hours, his heat warming her in the cool night. His heart beat fast, far faster than what she thought normal, but she clung to him and relished the feel of him, strong and hard, holding her like she weighed nothing at all. How could a man whom she had met less than twenty-four hours ago make her feel safer and more cherished than Frank—a man she had known her whole life?

When finally able to string a sentence together, she asked the first thing that came to mind, without lifting her head. "Why are you always naked when I find you?"

He chuckled. "Perhaps I'm waiting for you."

"Mmm." What if he always waited for her? Naked or dressed, it didn't matter. Oh, *who am I kidding?* Dana loved the way his muscles clenched under her fingers as she glided them over his back. So, if she had to vote, naked won.

"Are you all right?" His voice, soft against her wet hair, caressed her.

She took a mental inventory. She did appear to be in one piece though she wasn't sure she'd be able to walk straight for a week. But something inside seemed different, as if what they had done had changed her irrevocably. "I'm not sure."

He eased away to stare at her, his usually stern face marred with concern. "Did I hurt you?

"No, I think you healed me." Where the words came from, she had no idea, but once they'd been said, she wouldn't take them back. She finally felt like a woman, not frigid or asexual. That must be how Jessie felt when she had sex, and what Dana had never understood because she'd never experienced this mix of desire and lust before. Nor had she had an

66

orgasm like that, one that made her want to have sex again. Immediately.

"I'm no healer." Rekkus moved them toward the edge of the lake. Only then did he withdraw from her and lower her to her feet. Strolling over to the rock where he'd tossed his clothes, he handed her his T-shirt. "This should cover you."

Instinct warned her it might not fit, but she so wanted to feel it against her, be wrapped in his unique scent. She removed the wet blouse and bra and the old familiar feeling of insecurity crept over her. Now as naked as he was, knowing what her body looked like, she didn't want to imagine what someone like Rekkus, with abs like Michelangelo had chiseled, was used to in a woman. She clutched the fabric to her chest, afraid for a moment to try the top on.

"What's wrong?" He moved over to her, placed his palm against her cheek, and searched her eyes.

Biting her lower lip, she shook her head and spun away from him. How silly she must appear. But now, with her back to him, he had a perfect view of her full hips and fuller ass. She didn't want to see his face as she attempted to pull on the shirt only to discover what she'd feared; it didn't fit over her Rubenesque figure. Worse, she didn't have a choice, because her own clothes lay in a muddy, wet pile at her feet. But she couldn't stand here clutching the fabric to her breasts all night either.

Wordlessly, he helped arrange the T-shirt down her damp back and over her ass. Although snug, it managed to cover her. When she faced him, he had the same expression he'd worn when she had arrived earlier.

"You are so sexy. You have no idea what seeing you in that does to my baser need to make you mine forever."

Her breath caught. He didn't see her as overweight? How could this man want her so much? "I might get—what the hell is that?"

Rekkus swung away in enough time to see a young gray werewolf coming out of the wooded grove. The were's eyes were alight with the power of the moon, crazed in his inability to control his hormones.

"Damn it! Telly, you were supposed to lock yourself in the kennel tonight." But Rekkus's words fell on deaf ears as the wolf locked his sights on the yet-unmated female. Rekkus placed himself between the were and the woman he hoped would mate with him by week's end. Putting a hand behind him, he yanked her tightly against him, wanting to know where she stood when the young cub attacked.

Between the hormones and attitude flowing through immature shifters, they proved a danger to everyone around them. And a pain to control. Many para parents who lived in the modern world with humans had begun sending their adolescent shifters to the resort during the full moon. The young men stayed on the other side of the island, where a kennel had been erected to both house and hold them until the moon phase waned, making it safe to go home again.

For a few days every month, Telly came to visit. During the day, he acted like any normal para teen, active and showboating. But, when the moon rose, he became aggressive and downright mean. He'd attacked one of the handlers the prior month, and had Rekkus been in a state of mind to pay attention, he'd have remembered Telly required him to control him during this new-moon cycle.

"Whatever you do, stay behind me until I tell you to run, Dana," Rekkus warned. "Then run and don't stop until you reach the Haus. Do I make myself clear?"

"Yes." Her nails bit into his biceps, her obvious anxiety infusing him with a new, unfamiliar protective streak.

"Good." He kept one arm in front of him to block any attack that might come his way, and a hand on Dana because, if it came to it, he'd throw her in the lake. Serena was somewhere nearby, singing, something he'd deal with later. Without a doubt, if he called, Serena would come. The siren might have a thing about hurting men, but she had a soft spot when it came to women, and she'd protect Dana.

His plan to protect Dana forming in his mind, movement caught his eye as a second wolf made its approach.

"Damn it!" Rekkus snarled. Was every member of his team completely incapable or unable to control a pack of teenagers?

The second wolf lunged at the same time Telly did, giving Rekkus a split second to make the decision to shift. One adolescent shifter attacking him in human form caused no threat, and even the second posed little danger, but controlling their moon lust and protecting Dana...that he didn't trust. In animal form, he could take on whole packs while still protecting his mate.

He knocked the pouncing wolf away and without waiting for the second attack, shifted into a seven hundred pound black tiger. Larger than most shifters, Rekkus had more power than the two cubs could handle. With a growl, quickly followed by a hiss, he bared his teeth. Laying his ears back, he leaned on his haunches then lunged.

Normally, Rekkus played with the young cubs to teach them a lesson, but they'd put his mate in danger, and that he could never allow. Dana yelled, and he sensed her step away. Only then did he attack the wolves head on, batting one away with a paw, while still keeping his frame between them and Dana. The first pup yelped when Rekkus's claws raked his flank, rolling him away. The second howled and jumped, trying to gain leverage against his massive opponent.

Rekkus pinned it to the ground, and as the urge to rip its throat out came over him, Cyrus's voice came from behind. Cyrus had the first wolf by the scruff of the neck and had stretched out to seize the second, wounded pup by his scruff as well.

"Cemil, take one of these, please," Cyrus barked.

Cemil, stepping forward, fought with the animal for a moment, finally subduing him.

Though still furious, Rekkus took a deep breath, released the tension, and let the shift take him back to human form. The sound of the gamekeepers in the distance did little to ease his anger. He had put his lust and desire for Dana ahead of the safety of the island. When the gamekeepers approached, the fury on Rekkus's face had them stammering apologies.

Assured they'd be dealing with Rekkus in the morning, they took the animals from the Rowan brothers and left.

"That should never have happened," Rekkus said, lowering his face in an act of repentance. The submissive movement was unfamiliar, but he had failed not only the Rowans with his need to mate, but also the cubs.

Cemil didn't approach him in his normal way, and Rekkus assumed something in his demeanor must have told the other man safety lay a few feet away.

"This isn't your fault," Cemil said. "Your main priority has to be Ms. Stone. And I think she might need you about…now."

Rekkus spun just as Dana paled and her eyes rolled back. Cyrus and Rekkus rushed to catch her as she went down. When Cyrus reached her first and eased her to the ground, fury like nothing Rekkus had ever felt washed over him.

"It's okay, Rek, only helping out." Though Cyrus's tone was light, he still had the good sense to back off once Rekkus had his arms around her.

"You've got to complete the bonding ceremony before you rip someone's head off."

Rekkus shook his head and lifted her with ease. "I'll not force her to mate with me."

"I didn't say you'd have to."

Of everyone, only Cyrus understood the full depth of why Rekkus would never force any woman to be his mate. Nodding, he began the hike toward the main building while Cemil collected her discarded clothes and followed a safe distance behind them.

"You do know you are naked," Cyrus said.

"Yes."

"Just checking."

Rekkus cringed. *That* was not how he'd envisioned telling or showing Dana his true self. He had hoped to do it over time, by convincing her to stay on for more than a week then working up to the big reveal. Instead, she'd seen the worst of him, and of the shifting species as a whole. Damned full moon, and pups who had no idea how to control their baser urges. Honestly, Rekkus hadn't thought through how he planned to tell her about his kind, but *that* had not

74

been it.

Passing one of the hot tubs, he snatched a towel to better cover Dana. The thought of anyone else seeing her bare legs might send his loosely leashed beast into another rage. The best thing for the entire island was for him to get her safely to his room and shut the world out until they'd dealt with this issue, or at least until he had the possessive streak threatening to overtake him under control.

"You might want another towel." Cyrus laughed with a pointed look at Rekkus's bare ass.

He ignored him and continued on. He didn't care who saw him naked. His prime concern was not having Dana awake and freak out. He cared for no one else's reaction but hers. She'd undoubtedly be furious, upset, and confused, and he refused to add embarrassed to the list.

He nestled her against him, hoping she absorbed the protective energy he sent her.

Marching into the mostly empty lobby, he relaxed. The room at that time of the evening usually held a great many guests. He ignored the wide-eyed, open-mouthed Myron. In any other situation, he might have enjoyed the unshakable gypsy's shock, but instead only headed to the elevators.

"He's naked," she said in a whisper that might as well have been louder than a yell.

"He knows," Cyrus said.

"Does he want a blanket?"

"Apparently not."

Cyrus pushed the elevator call button for his friend and, when a couple of paras approached, he waylaid them in his normal, charming way. "I'd suggest taking the next lift."

Rekkus stormed to the rear of the elevator and rested against the wall. Dana began to moan, and his patience nearly failed him.

"Do you need me to open your door?" Cyrus asked.

"No."

"Good. Then I'll see you when your beast is in check. I'm heading to the kennels. I believe an extra set of hands will be appreciated down there tonight."

Once off the lift, Rekkus didn't stop until they

were in his room and he'd placed Dana with care in the middle of his king-size bed. After lighting the candles in the room, he found a blanket in the cedar chest under the bed and covered her. Then, he waited, sitting beside the bed before pacing, and finally doing what his heart demanded—he covered her body with his. When she relaxed into his embrace, he hoped the Fates knew what they were doing in that moment.

Chapter Five

Dana awoke, refreshed and relaxed. Her dreams had been pleasant enough, other than the super-bizarre dream involving having sex with super-hunky Rekkus, followed by him becoming a black cat-like beast. The sex part rocked her cavernous world, but the other part just seemed wrong.

She opened her eyes and the sunlight streaming through the soft sheers on the three windows collected the dust shimmering and dancing in the beams. The blanket seemed warmer and heavier than she remembered. Attempting to remove it, she came in contact with a large, strong arm. In slow motion, she rolled her head to find Rekkus sound asleep beside her, the slightest of snores coming from him. As she tried to ease his arm off her and exit the bed, he pulled her closer, refusing to let her leave.

Panic threatened to overwhelm her. All the blurry, dream-like images crashed over her like waves on a shoreline. The fear of the wolves, that Rekkus would be hurt, followed by shock and disbelief as he'd morphed from human to cat. Her brain fought what she had witnessed, but then she remembered Cyrus and Cemil Rowan coming on the scene, acting like that happened every day at the Wiccan Haus, controlling wolves as if they were puppies.

Still convinced she had seen it all wrong, Dana closed her eyes as she had earlier, when she'd first spotted the creature, but when she opened them, her lover still lay beside her. Her blood ran cold, and the room spun.

Panic escalated into an anxiety attack. Fighting his hold against her, she hadn't realized she'd hit him until he wrapped his fingers around her wrist, gentle, and unexpected.

"You'll hurt yourself, *fy nghariad*." He let go and inched away, giving her the space she both craved and hated. "Sit up, take a deep breath, and I'll get you some water."

"Put…clothes…on…please?" she gasped between gulps of air. Her brain and libido fought memories of the night before, and she feared she'd

79

lose her mind. Yet, her body screamed for his touch the farther away he moved. She shouldn't want to want him so much. She wished she could go back in time and pretend this vacation had never happened.

Unable to relax as he'd requested, she rocked in a fetal position by the time he returned. When he touched her shoulder, she jerked without meaning to. After handing her a bottle of water, he paced the room, much as a feline did.

"Oh my God. You're a tiger. And I don't mean in the 'grrr, you're a tiger in bed, you stud' way, but as in, 'holy shit you're a fucking tiger!'"

He halted, eased closer then must have seen something on her face because he stopped again. "I am."

"And you're human?"

"Yes."

"So, what are you? A werewolf, I mean tiger? What the hell is going on?"

"I'm of a race that is both man *and* animal." He took another tentative step. "Please let me hold you."

"Not yet. I can't think when you touch me."

Dana lifted two shaky hands, hoping that could keep him at bay. "So the others? They're really witches?"

"They're Wiccans, and they really do have powers."

"That isn't possible." She shook her head and waited for him to say something—anything—but she supposed he wasn't about to argue with the crazy lady. "Can you turn anytime you want?"

"I can."

"Do it." She frowned. "No, wait. Don't. Okay, um, sure, be the tiger. No, no, don't."

He stood across the room, head slightly down, eyebrows raised, and regarding her as though she'd lost her mind.

Well, guess what, mister? I did lose my mind, and you caused it.

"Dana?"

She'd deal with it and not hide. "You know what? I *do* want you to turn into whatever you are."

He blinked, surprised. "You want me to shift now?"

"Yes. Well, I think I do. You protected me last

night, so I assume you can control your animal self."

"I'll never hurt you." He made a move toward her and sighed when she jumped to the other side of the bed. Thinking a king-size bed between them protected her was silly, but something seemed better than nothing at the moment. If she'd had a whip and a cane chair, she would have used it.

She braced herself. On a deep inhale, he filled his gorgeous chest before removing the jeans he had put on at her request. Biting her lower lip, Dana witnessed him shift. Although it happened rather quickly, it hadn't been pretty and appeared to be painful. The sound of bones cracking had her jerking back. His gaze never left hers as a soft glow covered him, followed by the appearance of fur. The change started at his head, down his body, ending with a long tail. He made not a sound, as if the process didn't particularly faze him. Within a few seconds, Rekkus the human disappeared and a giant black-and-gray tiger had taken his place.

Even having seen the change, Dana had a hard time accepting this animal was Rekkus. He sat back on his haunches and waited, his big golden eyes staring at her. After what seemed like hours, Dana took a few tentative steps around the bed. Her heart beat so hard and fast, he had to be able to hear it. Her breathing became short and labored. Each measure brought her closer to the beast, and other than calmly inhaling and exhaling, he remained motionless. He had to be the largest cat she had ever seen, beautiful, majestic, and deadly. Only then did she notice his gray stripes were silvery.

Stretching tentative fingers toward the cat, she dropped them again. "Can I touch you? Can you understand me when you're shifted?"

She waited, and he rose and batted his head at her hand, his fur soft between her fingers. When he purred loudly, a laugh escaped her. He really was a bigger version of her kitty waiting for her at home.

In an awe-filled voice, she said, "You're gorgeous."

How many people ever got that close to an animal so large? Who'd believe this? This gorgeous man, who made love like a hero in an erotic novel, changed at will into the magnificent beast.

Strange, but, as large and dangerous as he obviously was, she had no fear. Instead, a sense of peace and protectiveness came over her. As Rekkus continued to purr and rub against her legs, she got a good opportunity to admire the amazing creature. His black fur, with its silvery stripes, gave him a majestic appearance, and made him all the more impressive. She'd never seen a black tiger, never known they existed, but then she'd never thought magic existed until the previous night.

"You can change back if you want."

The cat padded away from her, giving one soft bay then returned to human form. Rekkus, completely naked and glorious in all his natural beauty, stood before her.

"You can touch me now, too," he said, his voice cool and calm, though his golden eyes screamed with primal desire.

Easing away, Dana shook her head. "I don't think that's a good idea."

Rekkus grabbed his discarded jeans and yanked

them on. She tried not to whimper as inch by inch of glorious muscles were covered by the denim. He tugged a black T-shirt over his head.

"Does it hurt?" Striving for something coherent to say, she asked, "Does it hurt when you change?"

"When I *shift*. We call it shifting, not changing. We're not changelings. We can't become something we aren't, but we are able to shift into the other part of the being in our soul."

He sat on a nearby chair, and she knew he did it deliberately, to give her a sense of control, but it didn't help. That had to be a new role for him, being submissive, even if only for a minute or two, and only to let her feel more at ease. She stood over him, and he leaned back.

Placing both hands on his knees, he shook his head. "It's uncomfortable, but it doesn't hurt. It's much like a leg cramp, but not real pain. I don't even notice it anymore. Young shifters feel more discomfort."

It sure sounded painful.

"Oh." She couldn't think of anything else to say,

really.

"I understand this must be hard for you to accept."

"You could say that." Dana cleared her throat. "So, what else can you do?

He gave her a cheeky grin. "Do? Is this not enough?"

She rolled her eyes. "Yes, but I'm trying to gauge if there's more I should know."

"Tons more, but I only shift into one animal form, if that is what you are asking." He hesitated, as if thinking about how to word his next sentence. "No shifter can hurt you when you're with me. I want you to know that. I am stronger than most."

She'd figured that one out on her own. The way he'd dealt with the wolves the previous night gave her a good inclination of his power. "Did you change...um, I mean shift, last night because of the full moon?"

"No. That, along with allergies to silver and taking off with babies in the night is all Hollywood bullshit." Although his voice dripped with disgust,

Rekkus hadn't directed it at her, but rather at the way his kind had always been portrayed.

Dana worried her lower lip between her teeth. Too many questions swam in her head and she didn't know where to start. Beginning with the one that worried her the most, she asked, easing herself up onto the bed, "So, last night you said something about mating. What does that mean?"

"Wow, you do go right for the jugular, don't you?" Rekkus worked his hands through his hair, messing it into a charming tangle. "It means nothing for you. You aren't bound to me in any way, shape, or form."

"What about you?"

"You are not mated to me, but last night, under the full moon, I became your mate."

"But you said the full moon—"

"The moon didn't cause my shift." He went to stand but paused. "As you saw, I can shift whenever I choose. It does, however, affect us strongly."

He glanced at her, and his shoulders relaxed. She sensed he was neither used to answering questions nor particularly keen on it. But his patience with her encouraged her to continue. Taking a sip of water to buy time, she tried to digest the information. A new world she never imagined existed and weakened her knees. Sitting on the edge of the bed, she braced herself to ask the most important question.

"So, what does being my mate mean? I'm assuming we aren't talking friendship here?"

"Friendship is usually a plus, but no, I'm now, for lack of a better word, your *husband*, but you are *not* my wife. Not yet. That choice is yours, and yours alone. I won't lie. I can force the mating ritual, but I won't."

That was a relief, in an odd sort of way. "What happens if I don't *mate* with you?"

"Eventually, the Fates will choose another mate for me." The words seemed to be dragged begrudgingly from him.

"Really?" *Another mate? Over my dead body will another woman touch him.* And where the hell had that overpowering jealousy come from? She didn't want to be mated, did she?

88

"Really."

"I'm not saying I want to, but does mating require you to bite me and make me a shifter?"

He slumped against the back of the chair, obviously impatient with her assumption. "You watch too many movies. I cannot make you a shifter any more than you can make me a human. I don't bite—nip, maybe—but never harm you."

"Everything is moving so quickly. Three nights ago I stood at the altar, in front of a church full of people, about to say 'I do,' when the words 'I don't' came out of my mouth."

A measure of pain crossed Rekkus' face, and he ground out, "That must have come as a shock to the bridegroom."

Could the thought of her marrying another man bother him that much? "Only that I said it first, because he followed it by, 'I don't, either.' Within seventy two hours, I went from being engaged, with a large, though not-quite-loving family, to being disowned, unmarried, and on a bizarre island instead of on a Caribbean honeymoon. And I really doubt this island is actually off the coast of Maine."

The room seemed to be getting smaller. She stood and began to pace, rubbing sweaty palms on her shirt.

"Now, I'm here, and I supposedly have a mate who, though sexy as hell, is part animal. I'm trying to accept that the four individuals who run this place may actually be what they say they are and have magic powers. And I think I might be losing my mind."

Dana stared at her shaky hands. She might be very close to losing it in front of Rekkus, afraid the nervous breakdown she'd been working toward for months had arrived, full-force. Maybe all of this—the Wiccan Haus, Rekkus, shifting animals were all in her head and, when she awoke, it would be the day before the wedding.

Or even better, the day of the proposal, and she still had the ability to back out. For once, she'd go against her family's wishes before it was too late and *just say no*.

Rekkus wrapped his strong arms around her. She

sank against his chest, letting his heat blanket and protect her.

Thinking she only required a few seconds to collect herself, she was surprised when tears unexpectedly pooled and the emotions she'd buried for a lifetime released. The tears fell in big drops, soaking his shirt. She cried for the relationship she'd lost with Frank; not because she'd loved him as a lover, but as a friend. She cried because of the conditional love her parents had always doled out, and for her life, which made no sense at all. Finally because she had lost her grandmother's watch, and, in all of Dana's life, only her grandmother had truly loved her for *her*.

Chapter Six

"Breathe in, one, two, three, four. Hold it, one, two, three, four. Exhale, one, two, three, four...."

"What the hell are we doing here? I feel like I'm in a birthing class," Jessie said, her voice barely audible over the ocean waves.

"Shhhh, I'm learning to breathe. *Properly*." Dana fought a smirk. She felt silly. They'd been working on the exercises for a half hour, and, after spending thirty years inhaling and exhaling without a problem, she didn't feel she needed lessons.

"We *are* learning to have a baby." Jessie had moved into full-sarcasm mode, not the most conducive thing for relaxation.

"Would you stop and just do it?" Dana glanced toward the Haus for the fourth time. She'd left Rekkus less than an hour earlier and already missed him, although part of her remained scared silly of him and the other part still so aroused she couldn't think straight with his naked image continually filling her head. Since he seemed to be naked half the time, her imagination didn't have far to stray.

"What are you looking for, or should I say, who?

"What are you talking about?"

"I heard you were unconscious and carried into the lobby by a naked man last night. Myron told me about it when I went searching for you. She said something about *a ruckus* and a naked, gorgeous man, and a few interesting things about his anatomy" Jessie motioned with her head to the older couple in front of them. "But I won't go into that here. Oh, and you were curled in his arms."

"Will you please shut up?" Dana hissed.

"Must have been some earth-tilting sex to make you pass out." Jessie laughed and then tried to hide it with a cough when the class leader, Trixie, gave her a stare of reproach.

Dana filled her lungs again and went through the steps a handful of times then leaned toward Jessie and whispered, "Mind-blowing."

Jessie did cough that time. "Holy hell, I was joking. You actually got laid?"

"You sound surprised."

Ignoring the class, Jessie said, "Of course I'm surprised. So it was good?"

"You have no idea."

In a soothing tone, Trixie announced, "Okay, if everyone would lie on their mats, we will do the next series of exercises while focusing on the solar plexus chakra or your middle chakra...."

Dana snuck one more peek toward the Haus then settled on her mat again. The ocean breeze cooled her skin heated by the sun. She closed her eyes, letting the rays seep into her, relaxing her further. On another deep inhale, she held it, let it out, and doubted she had been so languid in years. She listened to the mantra of the waves hitting the small, sandy beach a few feet from them. Just what she needed, lying there and resting.

Any minute, she would fall into a deep trance, or maybe just asleep. The sun crept almost entirely behind a cloud, interrupting her near-slumber, and the accompanying cool breeze sent a shiver up her spine. Opening her eyes, Dana lifted a hand to protect them from any rays not hidden.

"Dana, come with me."

That's no cloud. Rekkus stood above her, his palm outstretched.

"What are you doing here?"

"I have someone you should to meet."

"Now? I'm learning to breathe."

"You know how to breathe." He extended the hand farther. "Please."

"Rekkus, there had better be a good reason for you to interrupt my class," Trixie muttered.

He growled. Dana glanced over in time to see the instructor pale and take a step back.

Dana let him pull her to her feet. "Stop growling at people. They'll think you have a bad temper."

"Umm…this must be the naked man I have heard so much about," Jessie said. Rekkus lifted an eyebrow at her. "Pity I missed last night, but he is still quite something, even dressed."

Dana shrugged. "Funny, I usually don't get to see him with his clothes on."

"Lucky."

"I'm right here, ladies." Rekkus marched off, dragging Dana behind him.

"Wait, you can't just take her with you," Trixie yelled. "She's not done yet!"

"The hell I can't." He strode full-speed to the Haus. Expecting and anticipating he would head into the resort to take her to bed, Dana squashed her disappointment when he led her toward a roped-off, wooded path with a sign that read *Staff Only*. She stumbled, trying to keep up with his long strides finally asking him to stop.

Turning, he started to say something, but instead licked his lips, let out a guttural noise, and kissed her. With no fight left in her, she opened her lips for him.

Dana didn't know why she'd fought him that morning anyway. Being away from him for even the small amount of time during class had put so much into perspective, how much she wanted him and missed him. She felt safe with him like she never had at any time or with anyone in the past. She didn't have to be strong around him. He was strong enough for them both.

He'd never made a comment about her weight. The opposite, in fact, telling her and showing her the night before how much he loved her body. She felt perfect around him. All the years of insults and belittling heaped upon her by her mother, the embarrassment Dana had assumed her father endured because of her, and the sense of inadequacy she'd had when standing next to her stick-thin model sister disappeared in his arms. To Rekkus, she was sexy, and the Fates had created her especially for him. If the Fates saw fit to give her this man, she'd be foolish not to follow their advice and hold on with both hands.

He pulled away, burning a trail of kisses down her neck. Her nerves jumped to life, and shivers shot through her. He backed her against a tree off the path, not quite hidden, but out of view of anyone not expecting to stumble across a couple getting it on in the woods.

His mouth never left her skin. He worked the top few buttons of her blouse then gathered and lifted her skirt until he reached the apex of her thighs. Her panties, already wet, ripped with ease. She arched, begging him to touch her there. He complied, pushing two fingers inside her while his other hand released another button, giving him access to her aching breasts. Easing the bra to the side, he latched his lips onto her nipple, sucking it to a hard nub.

His thumb circled her clit, and Dana tried to stifle a moan, but it escaped anyway. His chuckled response against her breast brought a loud sigh from her. He worked her into a breathless frenzy with his hands and lips. When his mouth left her breast, she opened her eyes to see the familiar hunger on his face.

Dropping to his knees, he forced her legs open, his gaze never leaving Dana's until he kissed her intimately with lips so warm and soft. His cheek nuzzled her thigh, and she closed her eyes again, letting her head fall. She wanted him, could not stop him. It didn't matter if someone found them with her against a tree and his head up her skirt. What they were doing right then was all that mattered.

Rekkus lifted her leg and rested it on his

shoulder, leaving her open and vulnerable to him. The tip of his tongue found her clit, first with a light caress, then with a full lick. When he nipped her, she yelped. Then, with strong fingers, he worked her inner muscles until her breath hitched and she lost all focus. When his tongue entered her, her knee threatened to give out. She panted and begged for his help, afraid she'd be unable to support her own weight much longer. Rekkus pressed a palm against her stomach, bracing her, forcing her to accept the pleasure he gave her. Dana relaxed and let the currents of pleasure take her to a place no one else but Rekkus could take her.

She didn't know how long he held her there, but, in the next moment of clarity, Rekkus stood beside her, looking like the proverbial cat who'd eaten the canary.

"You do taste as good as you look," he said, brushing his lips on hers.

"I don't think you dragged me out of my class and brought me all this way for that." Dana gave him her best cheeky grin. But, if that had been the reason, so much the better. On unstable legs, she rose on tiptoes and returned his kiss.

"No, it wasn't, and I promise one of these days I will make love to you in a bed." Rekkus laid a peck on her palm. "Come with me. I have someone for you to meet."

Dana couldn't imagine who she hadn't met yet. There were a few groundskeepers eating their lunch at a picnic table and, although they paused for a second as she and Rekkus approached, no one spoke and they soon resumed their conversations. It would seem having a guest back there might be surprising to them, but no one questioned Rekkus.

They entered a building that reminded her of military barracks with small, sparse rooms where the bed sheets were so tight a dime would bounce off them. Nothing of any interest or color lined the rooms. Every room door stood open, fitted with a bar. Once the door closed, someone must drop the bar into the horizontal position locking it tight.. They gave the doors a clunky feel, and she could only imagine, getting out of the cell would be virtually impossible.

Commotion and yelling came from the end of the hall. As they got closer, it became obvious the racket emanated from teenage boys playing video games. Rekkus entered the room and motioned for her to remain silent. Four boys, apparently unaware of their presence, continued to focus on the television screen. Only when Rekkus cleared his throat did they drop their game controllers and line up with amazing speed.

"Boys!"

"Yes, sir!"

Four pairs of eyes, two wide with fear, focused on Dana. Unsure what they had to fear from her, she threw Rekkus a confused glance. When she gave the wary boys a small smile, it seemed to make them all the more nervous. The other young men brought their attention to Rekkus with anticipation and no small amount of hero worship.

"Boys, meet my mate, Dana Stone."

She wondered if she should be offended by the high-handed announcement to the group. Yet, try as she might, she couldn't summon even a little irritation over the announcement, only a warm feeling of belonging.

"Dana, meet our adolescent guests, Ben, John, Joseph, and Telly."

Telly? Familiarity buzzed in her brain, begging her to remember where she'd heard the name before. And then it came to her—the wolf from the previous night. Except not a wolf, but a *werewolf*, and now he stood, young and scared and human again.

Rekkus, through his entire, cool demeanor, still bristled with anger.

"Ms. Stone, I'm so sorry if I scared you last night. I wanted to take a run and feel the wind through my fur. I didn't know you'd be there, or I never would have done it. It's just...I didn't know," Telly said.

Dana looked to Rekkus. She didn't understand. He had explained he wasn't the only shifter on the island, but, until then, she'd never thought they truly existed.

"Dana, I promise Telly and the other boys will be securely locked in tonight. I'll be doing it personally at sunset."

Moans filled the room, and, although the kids weren't happy with the idea, no one seemed willing to fight Rekkus on the issue. They appeared so pathetic, for a second Dana thought about begging for leniency. Then she remembered the crazed glint they'd had and kept her mouth shut. After Rekkus told the boys he'd return in a few hours for lockdown, he and Dana left the building, hand in hand.

"I thought you said the moon doesn't affect your shift?" This whole shifting thing confused the hell out of her.

"It doesn't affect my shift, nor does it affect most adult shifters. But like any teenagers who can't control their hormones, they are influenced by the lunar phases. Between the moon's pull and their raging hormones, teen shifters can be unwieldy. Until last night, I felt sorry for them." His golden eyes darkened, and he squared his shoulders in anger.

She leaned into him, sensing it would calm him, slowing their pace as the weight of his words sank in. "You mean, until they went after me."

"Nothing can happen to you. Do you understand? For me, knowing you are safe is tantamount to survival. Without that, I'll go insane. That doesn't mean you're stuck here with me. You're free to go live your life back on the mainland, but I have to know that, no matter what, you're safe."

"I don't consider staying with you being stuck." Instead, she had a strong desire to stay and get to know this man better.

Rekkus stopped and pulled her around to face him. This was too important for him not to see her face. "What are you saying?"

"I'm saying—and maybe it's too soon to say, but, for now, I'd like to stay here. Maybe I can do some odd jobs on the island. I don't have a job to go home to, no home actually. I have to make some money to pay off my parents for all they spent on my wedding. I can't leave them with that bill."

"I think we can arrange something." His head swirled with images and ideas. He'd move Heaven and Hell to get her to stay with him. However, he also smelled her fear, especially the uncertainty that everything moved too fast. Humans required time, courting. Paras required no time at all. They sensed their mate immediately. Some fought it, as he had, but they knew. Humans, on the other hand, rarely listened to what their souls told them.

"I'd need a place to stay."

"I could get us a cabin." There was no real way to get the housing situation to work at the big Haus. Not with the elevators. Not even for him would they change the rule against paras on the third floor, and Dana couldn't use the elevator to his.

"I like the sound of us."

But, the scent of nervousness still rose off her in waves. She needed his reassurance. So many years of damage to her spirit couldn't be mended in a week. He hoped for both their sakes he never met her family. They didn't deserve her.

Wrapping his arms around her, he said, "Come on, let's head back, and I'll see about that cabin for us. I think they're all full this week, but, next week, there should be an opening."

As they strolled, he reveled in the way she leaned into him, grasped him tighter when they approached someone, or just smiled at him. Nearing the Haus, she blushed as people stared at them, unaware they were staring because of his actions, not her. They had never seen a soft side of him, so it raised a few eyebrows.

Myron didn't even glance up from her cards. "Sarka wants to see you alone, Rekkus, and Sage wants to see Dana in her garden."

"Sorry, luv." Rekkus said to Dana. "I never argue with the boss lady. I'll find you later."

"Why does Sage want to see me?"

"That's hard to say, but with Sage there is nothing to fear."

He kissed her, fighting the need to follow as she walked out of the Haus. He no longer experienced the same anxiety he'd had that morning, watching her leave, only the desire to be with her.

"She has accepted you," Cemil said in a soft tone.

"Cemil," Rekkus acknowledged and continued to

keep his gaze on the empty doorway. But a part of him eased at his friend's four simple words. If Cemil sensed her acceptance, then it was more than wishful thinking on Rekkus's part.

"She doesn't know it yet, but her soul has accepted you also." Cemil offered the answer to the question Rekkus never asked. "Sarka is climbing the walls with worry. She's terrified you are about to leave the island with your mate." Cemil didn't phrase it as a question, but Rekkus sensed Cemil worried as well. Rekkus would have to have a long chat with the Rowans about what his word meant.

When he entered the room, Sarka rose—paused—then sat again. "Took you long enough."

"I found out you wanted to see me less than a minute ago."

"So, is she staying, or are you leaving?"

"Cut to the chase, Sarka." Rekkus leaned against the bookshelf facing her desk.

"I don't have time to pussyfoot around this. Well?" Sarka's voice rose.

For all of two seconds, Rekkus thought about

making her suffer. A bigger pain in the ass didn't exist, but her worry came from love. "I am staying. Even if Dana leaves, I will continue to protect Cyrus and the rest of you. So, I will not leave the island."

Sarka let her head drop with relief and sighed. "Thank you. I'd never ask you to stay if your mate left, but I don't know what we'd do without you."

"By the Goddess, you will never have to find out."

"I think a cabin will suit you best. You can't bloody well stay here. We can have one ready for you both on Sunday. Perhaps build something bigger later." Sarka rounded her desk, grabbed Rekkus's left hand, and, from his pinkie, removed the copper ring his sister had given him as she died. Before he could say anything, she took another, hideously ugly ring with a brown rock set in it from her drawer then dropped both rings into a bowl. After pouring a foul-smelling liquid over them, she covered the bowl with a silk cloth. Then she began to chant. The air around them seemed to thicken as she spoke, her voice deep yet soft. Circling her hand over the bowl, she closed her eyes.

Rekkus waited, knowing better than to make a sound. The bowl glowed orange from inner heat, and smoke sifted upward. After a time, the scent of sulfur filled the room. Removing the fabric, Sarka poured water from a pitcher over the glowing-red rings, which hissed as they cooled, then she positioned her hands on either side of the bowl. Careful not to touch them, Sarka pulled the jewelry out with the silk rag and then rubbed them a few times before laying them in Rekkus's palm. He stared at the now-silver rings. A purplish rock had supplanted the brown one in the smaller of the transmuted metal circles.

"Lepidolite is the stone of protection, love, and self-healing. It will protect Dana when you can't. It will surround her with calm. The silver will help conduct the stone's power from you to her. Not, I realize, normal wedding rings, but I think you'll find your mate will be thrilled with them."

Sarka, who Rekkus had known for as long as he'd known Cyrus, had never once offered her powers to him. In fact, he'd never seen her use her powers. He only knew she was a powerful witch whom the Syndicate feared. He also suspected she alone used the first elevator, but he never broached that topic. When they had first acquired the island, she'd requested a room that only she could go into. Once he'd ensured the room's safety in the basement of the Haus, Rekkus had never again set foot in it. And when he needed to go down there, he and his security detail used the stairs.

"She will love it." The moon's pull alerted him to its rise above the ocean edge. "I have to go. I have some pups to secure for the night."

"They pose no threat to her now. You do know that?"

"Yes, but they do pose a threat to themselves," Rekkus said before heading toward the barracks. He had too much to take care of without worrying about adolescent pups. He'd make sure they were locked down to within an inch of their lives.

As he left the Haus, he looked to Myron. "Could you wire from my account whatever amount your cards tell you Dana owes her parents. Dana's friend,

Jessie, should have the address."

Once outside, he paused for a minute, breathing in the sweet dusk air, and shifted. Then he ran toward the fading light and the howling pups.

Chapter Seven

Dana stood quietly as Sage cultivated her garden, not wanting to disturb the woman who molded the plants the way an artist blended paint on a pallet. Dana loved gardening, had spent many summers with her grandmother in the mountains of North Carolina, weeding the older woman's nursery. Flower and vegetable alike had gotten such loving care under her gram's green thumb. Even in the city, Dana managed to grow her own cooking herbs and a few tomatoes.

"Dana, you're welcome to join me." Sage handed her a pair of bright-pink gloves. "I try so hard to keep up with this, but much of the time I feel it gets away from me."

"It's a beautiful garden."

Sage changed the subject. "You have decided to stay with us?"

No longer taken aback by the siblings' powers of observation, Dana nodded. "Yes. I'm not sure how long it will last, but I'm staying for now."

"Ah, I see." Sage pulled off her gloves, adjusted her skirt then sat on the ground so she and Dana could chat. She motioned for Dana to sit. This woman seemed wise beyond her years. "Do you know why Rekkus is here on this island with us?"

Dana shook her head.

"Rekkus came with us when we acquired the island, but he'd been, and still is, Cyrus's bodyguard. He is our guardian, appointed by the Syndicate to protect this island and those on it."

"The Syndicate?"

"The governing body for paras. Think of it like the Supreme Court. They make the rules by which we all abide. They govern as well as keep the order and the peace."

"And this Syndicate appointed Rekkus to guard Cyrus?" Having seen Cyrus only a handful of times, Dana couldn't understand why a man like him would need a bodyguard.

"They did. And until you came along, I never saw Rekkus flounder. Never once was there a security breach. Until last night."

"Are you saying you want me to leave?"

"No, quite the opposite. I hope you stay, but you must accept what your soul has already come to terms with. You have found your soul mate and he, you."

"It's all happened so fast."

"How much time does a soul require to know it has found its other half? I know our world is different than what you are used to."

"Not so different."

Cyrus entered the walled-in area but stayed at the other end. Dark in appearance, in contrast to his sister's lighter one, of the four siblings only he wore conventional clothing and short hair. If not for Rekkus, Cyrus would have caught her fancy. And possibly intimidated the crap out of her, too.

"What do you know, brother?" Sage asked, gathering her blonde braid and throwing it over her shoulder.

Cyrus drew closer to them. "The watch, the one that led Rekkus to Ms. Stone the first day; Rekkus asked me to touch it to find its owner." He met Dana's glance. "It belonged to your grandmother, didn't it?"

"Yes, she gave it to me when she passed."

"She was a witch. Her power brought soul mates together."

"She was a matchmaker," Dana agreed, "but she wasn't a witch."

"Perhaps, but she had power. I sensed it in the timepiece. I tried to warn Rekkus, but, as always, he blew it off." Cyrus squatted in front of her. Lifting her chin, he forced her to look into his icy-blue eyes. "You must go to him of your own will. He'll never force you and he'll never push. His father forced his mother, and she eventually went mad, killing the entire black tiger streak in one evening."

Sage tsked. "Cyrus, she isn't ready to know all this."

"She must know why Rekkus will never ask her to mate. She has to understand why he is the last of his kind, that he's a part of our family and so will she be."

Sage nodded and grabbed Dana's hand. "Very well, tell her everything, for Rekkus's sake."

"The black tiger shifters had been dying out for centuries. Only recently, in the last few decades actually, someone discovered shifters could mate with humans. A few mated with other weres, but when they did, the cubs were all of the golden streak."

"Streak?" Dana asked, confused.

"Streak is like a pack for tigers. There are a few species within golden, orange, white, but also black. As you have seen, that is the family Rekkus belongs to," Sage filled in. "Continue, Cyrus."

"When Rekkus was born with all the traits of a full Duteigr Alpha, his father, the Alpha—" Cyrus smiled and answered Dana before she could ask the obvious question. "King of his people, the Alpha pushed his mother into the mating ritual, forcing the bond to happen. She broke, not all at once, but little by little."

"Why would she break?"

Despair and pain washed over Cyrus. He clenched his jaw and swallowed hard. When he seemed unable to answer, Sage reached for him. "Cyrus had the unfortunate task of investigating the murders. He was more affected by it than any other crime scene he'd had to work."

Sensing she was treading on sensitive ground, Dana said, "You don't have to answer that."

"She broke because humans are sometimes a weaker species," Sage said, as if that answered everything. "Go ahead, Cyrus."

"The queen called Rekkus home that night, but I had been attacked by rogue assassins, and Rekkus missed the family dinner. Luckily, he arrived late, but walked in to find his entire family dead or dying—she had poisoned them all. She'd waited at the table, surrounded by her family, and tried to convince Rekkus to eat. When he refused, she came after him with a knife."

Sage snorted. When everyone's attention fell on her, she acted surprised. "Sorry, but the idea that anyone would go after Rekkus with a knife...so ridiculous. The Fates gifted him with strength, and everyone knows it."

"Shall I continue?" Cyrus didn't wait for an answer "I don't know what happened, but I do know

117

he tried to save his siblings, yet it was too late. His mother killed herself later that night. Forty-seven members of his family were lost by her hand."

Sage squeezed her hand. "Dana, you have to know before his father died, just days earlier, he'd made Rekkus promise not to force a mating on any woman. That if he had to do it all over again, he wouldn't have forced his mother." She smiled. "Until you came here, he vowed never to mate with anyone, but when your soul screams for another, it's hard not to listen."

"Don't rush it, but when the time comes to bind your souls, you will have to ask him. He will not ask you." Cyrus stood, but instead of leaving, added, "He needs you, and I think you need him."

Chapter Eight

Three of the happiest days of her life came and went. Dana spent most of the time in Rekkus's arms. She visited him while he worked, in tiger form, with the wolf cubs. He taught them to control their shifts and how to protect themselves. His shift no longer bothered her and, when he finally admitted his need to swim shifted, she went with him.

His love for the boys he mentored on the island shone though. Knowing what had happened to his younger siblings, Dana understood his desire to take care of the younger ones. She even allowed her thoughts to drift toward what kind of father he'd be.

While he worked security around the island, she tended the garden with Sage. No longer did she have to go to the classes. She felt more at home with the staff than she had ever had with her own family. Even Jessie agreed Dana should stay on the island. The scheduled ferry would arrive in the morning, taking Jessie and ten other guests to the mainland, although

Jessie agreed to take care of Dana's cat at home and bring him with her when she came back to visit. They had already said their good-byes because Dana hadn't been sure if she would make it to the dock in time to see her off. During their good-byes, Jessie let slip Rekkus had paid Dana's parents the money she owed them, and Jessie had relished telling them what an amazing man Dana had found.

And, for the first time, the thoughts of her family didn't sting so much. With Rekkus, the past hurts didn't affect her at all. Looking around his room, boxed up and ready to move to the cabin set aside for their sole use, Dana wondered how a man could live in the space for five years and only have three boxes to show for it. She had been there one week and had two very large suitcases.

She pulled out a white lacy teddy from her honeymoon bag she'd somehow managed to miss. When her plans had changed from tropical island as newlyweds, to island spa with a friend, she had unpacked anything remotely sexy, or so she'd thought. She wanted to make the night special or, at the very least, let she and Rekkus get to the bed and make love. So far they hadn't succeeded. They'd made it as far as the floor, the wall, the steps leading to the bed, the chair, and even the shower. Tonight, he wasn't leaving this bed until they had made love in it.

Kneeling on the firm mattress, Dana waited. The hairs on her nape alerted her of his approach, and excitement coursed through her as the door opened. Wearing his usual black T-shirt, pants, and work boots, he purred when he spotted her. He advanced, dragging his shirt over his head.

"You have the worst timing, luv,'" he said, yanking off one boot then the other.

On all fours, she edged to the end of the bed. "Why is that?"

"The paras leave at sunrise, and I have to get the pups through the portals at sunset tonight to their parents."

"Mmm, why can't they wait until morning with the rest of the group?"

"Have you ever tried to wake a teenager before noon?"

If she had her way, they'd never leave their room until after lunch either. Coming up to greet him, she sucked one nipple, moving toward his face, kissing as she went, first his neck and then the place below his ear that drove him crazy. His arm snaked around her waist, drawing her close.

"Sounds likes you have plenty of time to have your way with me."

"Never enough time," he growled.

"Always enough time." Dana tugged him down onto the bed with her. Focused on his belt buckle, she jerked it free, throwing it across the room. Next, she tackled the button-fly jeans. Eager fingers made quick work of the five buttons until they released enough for her to push his pants over his hips and rounded ass.

His mouth found hers again. He helped her ease the jeans the rest of the way off, and she reveled in the sound of the fabric hitting the floor and the feel of his bare skin where it touched hers. The hair on his chest tickled her nipples through the silk teddy and, when Rekkus drew her hips more intimately against his, she whimpered. His hard cock rubbed her through the soft material, and she nearly cried in frustration. He rewarded her with another long, slow grind before easing away to admire her.

"As sexy as you are with this on, it must come off. Now." He didn't have to explain that either she removed it or it would be in pieces when he did it for her. She'd bemoaned the fact that a great many panties had been ruined because of his impatience, and he'd promised to try and curb his excitement—a promise he'd managed to keep about half the time.

Dana rose to her knees and took her time letting the first strap fall off her shoulder. The hunger in his golden eyes ignited into flames. Slowly, so much like his tiger form, he sauntered around the bed until he stood behind her, nuzzling her bare shoulder. One hand settled on her hip, and the other cupped her breast through the silk. She let her head fall against him.

"You are so perfect," he said against her neck.

In truth, he made her feel perfect. Perhaps the Fates had known they were perfect for each other.

She transferred her attention to the other strap, leaving her upper torso bare to him. Her breasts fell free, and the nipples peaked in the cool air. Small goose pimples covered her as his warm hands kneaded her breasts.

She turned her face with a silent plea and, as always, Rekkus seemed so in tune with her, he didn't miss a beat. Climbing onto the bed, he kissed her then urged her onto all fours. He eased the rest of the teddy over her hips and thighs until it pooled at her knees. Dana glanced over her shoulder to find him focused on her ass. He gently rubbed circles over the pale skin.

With a light tap on her ass, he encouraged her to open wide for him. He settled between her legs, his knees pinning the fabric, binding her where she kneeled.

When he smacked her ass again, but with more force, the stinging sensation took her by surprise. Then it faded, replaced by a hot hand covering the sensitive skin. Moisture pooled at the apex of her thighs in response. This time, when his palm landed on her butt, it stole her breath, but she was ready. He repeated the action two more times his until the cheek burned and stung. But nothing could have prepared her for how his lips on the heated skin would feel.

It took every fiber of her being to control the oncoming orgasm. He blew gently on the stinging area, causing goose bumps to form, and his hands brushed to cool the fire. She gasped, unprepared when he struck the other ass cheek, but the surprise only lasted for a moment when the tingling sent ripples of pleasure through her.

"You have the sexiest ass I have ever seen," Rekkus said, his voice rough and heavy with passion.

She doubted he expected a verbal response, so she shook her hips enough to gain a moan from him. Gripping her hips, he buried his cock to the hilt. He filled and stretched her. In that position, he gained a depth she hadn't thought possible. But, by then, she knew him. He controlled his animal instinct to take her however he wanted. Instead, he clutched her hips, so tight they'd wear the marks of his restraint in the morning. Dana didn't care. They were meant for each other. Their souls needed this.

Dana inhaled and edged forward a few inches then shoving backward on his cock again. Motionless, he allowed her to create the rhythm. Allowing her control never lasted long. Dana continued the slow pace, knowing from their past encounters it drove him crazy. She savored the control while she had it, craved the sounds of pleasure he made, but, soon, his grasp would tighten and he'd take the reins.

Clutching the bedspread, she lowered her shoulders to the mattress, offering him full submission, letting him know she trusted him, that she'd be okay with him taking her his way. As soon as her cheek hit the cool sheet, he drove into her. He retreated only to return with more power. There was no beauty to his rhythm. no gracefulness to the passion, but he showed his supremacy and strength, and he carried her to heights she hadn't known existed.

The first waves of pleasure wracked her body then broke around her more powerfully than anything she'd experienced. Dana tried to catch her breath but could only pant. Rekkus didn't let up. His relentless pursuit of their pleasure offered no time-out. When she screamed out her second orgasm, she was done. But he pushed her, demanded she give him one more. That time she could only whimper as lightning shot through her, starting in her lower belly and sending shock waves through her limbs. Her legs quivered like jelly, and only because of his grip did her ass remain in the air. Then he roared, frozen, his cock jerking with the force of his orgasm as his pleasure poured deep into her.

Collapsing together, they curled around each other. Eventually, Dana rotated toward him, allowing Rekkus to lay his head between her breasts, eyes closed, both replete, his breathing calming. She ran her fingers through his soft hair and listened to him purr. She loved that about him, his purr the one thing that always reminded her he had a tiger within.

Dana watched him sleep in her arms for a long time. Even in slumber, he held her snug and cared for her. She belonged to him, to the Wiccan Haus.

Finally, she said, "You need to get out of bed if

you're going to get those pups home."

He lifted his head for a second but snuggled back against her breasts. "Five more minutes."

"Come on, big boy. The sooner you get this done, the sooner you can return to this bed with me."

Rolling to his back, he yawned then sat up, wiping his face. Dana loved the way he moved with the grace and elegance of a ballet dancer, something she wouldn't have thought possible for a man of his size. He faced her, as if knowing she watched him, and smiled. Then, in a gentle action, he tugged the sheet over her nakedness and stood to begin the search for his clothes.

"I've asked Sage to get some things from the mainland for you when she sends her shopping list with the ferryman tomorrow."

"She told me—said you requested sexy underwear."

"Well, yours are in short supply."

She wasn't going to mention if he'd stop ripping them off her, she'd have more than enough. "Mmm hmm. Jessie said she will mail me my stuff when she goes to my parents' house next week."

"Speaking of your parents, I sent them the money to pay off your wedding debt."

"I know. Jessie mentioned it. She isn't good with secrets."

"I hope you don't think it high-handed of me, but I have the money. I never spend it, and I didn't want that hanging over your head. Even with the job Sage gave you in the gardens, you'd never be able to pay them off."

"I think you're sweet. Thank you for worrying about me. Maybe one day they'll come around and you can meet them."

Dragging his pants back on, he sat on the edge of the bed with such an expression of devotion it took her breath away. He leaned over, kissed her lips, and then nipped her bare hip. "For you, I hope they do. But, to be honest, it's best if I never meet them because it will be very hard for me not to give them a piece of my mind."

She thought about it for a second and knew a piece of his mind wasn't all he'd like to give them.

The likely chance they'd ever set foot on the island seemed so remote it bordered on farcical. Her grandmother, on the other hand, would have loved this place and Rekkus, simply because he so obviously cared for Dana.

"I wish you could have met my grandmother. You'd have liked her."

"Oh, I almost forgot." He reached into his pocket and brought out a metal object. "I found it in the elevator tonight."

"My grandmother's watch!" Disbelief washed over her. "I thought I'd lost it for good this time."

He shrugged. "This is the second time I found the damned thing. I'll have Sarka check the clasp in the morning. I'd hate to have you lose it again."

Dana rubbed the crystal with the ball of her thumb. Come to think of it, both times she had tried to leave Rekkus, or ignored him, she'd lost the timepiece. Even from beyond the grave, her grandmother had made one final match, ensuring her beloved granddaughter had found her soul mate.

Then, suddenly, it became clear—Dana loved

Rekkus. Her grandmother had somehow known where Dana had needed to go and had gotten her there. Now, Dana had to take a leap of faith.

Swallowing around a lump, she said, "I won't lose it again."

"The odds are not in your favor." He chuckled.

"No, really. My watch, this watch, won't leave me because I won't leave you. My grandmother chose you as my match." The certainty of the situation grew stronger as she spoke the words.

He raised an eyebrow, as if Dana had lost her mind. "I suppose anything is possible."

Throwing herself into his arms, she kissed him, as if it were the last caress on earth. Leaning away, she stared up at him, loving him until her heart nearly burst with it. "Marry me, mate, do the binding thing. Whatever it is, I know this is right. I love you."

He froze then said with words coming from him on a whisper, "Say that again."

"I love you?" she teased. Although words of love were important for him, mating was everything, and yet, just as she'd been warned, he'd never once asked her. "Mate with me," she repeated.

" Are you sure?" He eased away. "Are you really sure?"

More certain than she had been about anything in her life. "Yes. How do we bind ourselves to one another? Do we have to wait till the full moon?"

"No, because I already bound myself to you then. You're human, so you can bind to me whenever you wish."

"So, what do I have to do?"

"When I kiss you, let your soul come to me, become my equal and my partner. Let *my* soul surround us. When you feel like you can't breathe, trust me and trust yourself."

"Okay." Could it be as simple as trusting him?

Rekkus brought her body into contact with his. Intertwining their fingers, she touched her lips to his. He gripped her almost painfully as a near-electrical current ran through them. She didn't know how she knew, but he was fighting the urge to shift.

Kissing him deeper, she took a full breath and held it. As he'd promised, his soul surrounded them, searching, hunting for hers. She allowed hers freedom, and it reached for his. She exhaled on a rush, as though her life were ending, and she panicked for a moment. Rekkus squeezed her hand gently, reminding her he would never let her fall.

A sense of calm came over her then. Opening her eyes, she found him staring, the awe she felt reflecting back at her from his gaze.

He released her and cupped her cheeks. *"Fy nghariad."*

He had said those very words to her many times, but this time they took on a depth of meaning she couldn't understand. "What does that mean?"

"My love."

She liked that. A lot. "So, that was it? We're mated?"

"Is that not enough? Did you not feel our souls bind?"

"Don't we need to howl at the moon or something?"

He snorted. "You and your damned movies. If you would prefer, after the teenagers have left, we

133

can go howl at whatever moon is left, to your heart's content." When he went to the dresser, she followed, touching the tattoo on his shoulder.

"I love this tattoo. Do all of your kind get inked like this with their species, or are you special?" She traced the intricate lines so perfectly inked in his skin.

He tensed beneath her fingers. "I suppose you can say I am unique. Very few of us have a tattoo like this, and yes, each species has its own version."

"You don't like talking about it, do you?"

He met her gaze in the dresser mirror. "I have talked more to you this week than I have to anyone my entire life. It is against my nature and I am conscious that you have questions that need answering."

She brushed her lips against the tribal marking. "You can tell me when you are ready."

"*Diolch yn fawr*. Thank you, luv."

"How do you say 'you're welcome' in Welsh?"

He smiled and pivoted to face her. *"Eich bod yn croesawu."*

Dana repeated what he'd said, knowing darn well

she butchered his beautiful language. She would work on it, wanting to know what he said when he spoke with some of his men, and she longed to understand his words to her in the heat of the moment. She suspected it would curl her toes.

He removed a red-silk handkerchief from the top drawer. "I do have something for you that might ease your human side. Nothing is more binding than our mating ritual, but if you require a human ceremony, I will—"

"I don't want a big ceremony." She was done with big glitzy weddings for the sake of wearing a white dress and entertaining people she could care less about.

"We are more married now than any paper on the mainland could make us, but Sarka fashioned these for us as wedding bands." He opened the red silk and laid the rings in her palm.

Nothing could have been more beautiful or perfect for Dana. As she held them, a sense of peace and calm filled her. After she gave the smaller ring back to him, Rekkus took a deep breath and slipped the band on the fourth finger of her left hand.

"I take you as my wife and my mate. My lover and my partner, until the moon ceases to rise." Simple and yet perfect.

She stared at the other ring she still clutched. He surprised her by holding out his left hand, and she slid it home.

"I make you my husband. You are my world and my rock. I will love you all the days of my life."

A knock at the door interrupted them. With reluctance, she let Rekkus, her *husband*, answer it. He spoke with someone in low tones then returned with a bottle of wine.

"Apparently, when we did the binding, my electrical current blew a few fuses, alerting the paras to what had happened. Cyrus said he will see the pups off safely. Everyone else said they do not want to see us until tomorrow morning, until after the ferry departs. They plan to throw us a wedding brunch."

"That's sweet." Everyone had been so accepting of her. His men treated her as though she walked on water. The siblings embraced her as one of the family. Even Sarka had given her a rare smile and welcomed her to the island. Dana had a sense of belonging she'd never had, even with her own kin.

"More like annoying. I would much rather spend the day in bed with you, my mate."

"I think I could be persuaded," she said in the sexiest voice she could summon. "Except we have to move down to the beach tomorrow."

"Fear not, I want nothing more than to get away from this building and to the seclusion of the lagoon." He advanced toward her. The clear intent in his gaze had her stepping back until her bottom came in contact with the bed. Once he'd lifted her onto the mattress, they were chest to chest. "It should allow us a bit more space."

"At least one could hope." For an island full of secrets, it offered little in the way of privacy. Everyone seemed to know her business before she did.

Laying her back on the bed, he climbed up next to her, half covering her body with his. Nuzzling her neck, he whispered, "In case I forgot to mention it, I love you, too."

About the Author

Award-winning author Dominique Eastwick grew up a US Navy Brat, so if there was a naval base, that was probably home. She currently resides in North Carolina with her husband, two children, crazy lab and lazy cat.

Dominique's love of reading started when she was told to read *To Kill a Mockingbird* in high school—a book that opened her eyes to the joys of reading and entering into the world of the author. To this day she ranks this book as her favorite.

Other Books by This Author

Strawberry Kisses

The Duke and the Virgin

The Marquis and the Mistress

The Earl and His Virgin Countess

Siren's Serenade

Healing His Soul's Mate

Infiltrating Her Pack